Sand Dollar Summer

Sand Dollar Summer

Kimberly K. Jones

ALADDIN MIX
NEW YORK   LONDON   TORONTO   SYDNEY

ALADDIN MIX
Simon & Schuster Children's Publishing Division
1230 Avenue of the Americas, New York, NY 10020
Copyright © 2006 by Kimberly K. Jones
All rights reserved, including the right of reproduction in whole or in part in any form.
ALADDIN PAPERBACKS and related logo are
registered trademarks of Simon & Schuster, Inc.
ALADDIN MIX is a trademark of Simon & Schuster, Inc.
Also available in a Margaret K. McElderry hardcover edition.
Designed by Krista Vossen
The text of this book was set in Berthold Baskerville.
Manufactured in the United States of America
First Aladdin Paperbacks edition June 2008
4 6 8 10 9 7 5 3
The Library of Congress has cataloged the hardcover edition as follows:
Jones, Kimberly K., 1957–
Sand dollar summer / Kimberly K. Jones.
p. cm.
Summary: When twelve-year-old Lise spends the summer on an island in Maine with her
self-reliant mother and bright–but oddly mute–younger brother, her formerly safe world is
complicated by an aged Indian neighbor, her mother's childhood friend, and a hurricane.
ISBN 978-1-4169-0362-8 (hc.)
[1. Islands–Fiction. 2. Family life–Maine–Fiction. 3. Passamaquoddy Indians–Fiction.
4. Indians of North America–Maine–Fiction. 5. Maine–Fiction.] I. Title
PZ7.J720455San 2006
[Fic]–dc22
2005012740
ISBN 978-1-4169-5834-5 (pbk.)

For Chuchi and Zoom-Zoom

and the memory of their father,

Robert R. Churchill

• *Acknowledgments* •

A novel, particularly a first novel,
is never published without many mercies, known
and unknown. Thanks to Bill Reiss for taking a chance
and being patient, and to Karen Wojtyla for shepherding
a novice painlessly through the process.
The Bridge School "older writers" served as a
gracious and gratifying first audience.
Blessings on you all.

The sea gives, and the sea takes away. The sea gave me a great deal, but fickle as it is, it tried to steal it back, and nearly me with it.

I had never been to the ocean before the year I turned thirteen. Until then I had grown up landlocked, where the only nearby water was a municipal swimming pool that burned my eyes red and turned my hair green. My brother and I lived with our mother in a safe, snug triangle: Mom was the base, and my brother and I were the sides that balanced upon her. We laughed a lot then, and I expected to go on that way forever, but the balance shifted suddenly, and everything changed.

Sand Dollar Summer

Chapter 1

My brother is not your standard brother. Free is beautiful. I don't mean he is cute in the way all little kids are cute, I mean he is gorgeous. He has blond, blond hair that curls around his face, and eyes a shade of gray green I've never seen on anyone else. Free has read since he was three, played piano since he was four. My friends Rachel and Elizabeth say their younger siblings are just pains in the butt, but I think Free is cool. We play Monopoly and cribbage and backgammon together, and he's a wicked chess player. He laughs, he cries, and he hums, but he does not talk. Free is five. Mom and I talk to Free just like normal, and somehow we always know what's on his mind. When people finally realize that he isn't just supershy, they ask me why he doesn't talk. I tell them the truth: I don't know, and I don't care.

When we moved to this neighborhood a year ago, kids on the block called him a freak and yelled things at him, as if he didn't hear instead of speak. Those kids were a little surprised at how fast I was and how hard I could hit for a skinny girl. And if their parents called and complained, Mom made mincemeat of them real quick. Nobody messes with my mom. At least more than once.

We had moved three times in five years and I was sick of it. Sick of being the new kid and just about finding someone I could be my real self with, and then boom! Mom would get a better job and move us someplace else. I'd tried crying and screaming at her, but Mom would just hold me and rock me and pat my back. "I have to do what I have to do," she'd say. I guess we were all sick of it, because this time she'd promised we'd stay for at least five years. Pinkie-promised.

When they tested Free for kindergarten, they didn't let him in.

"He's not quite ready for us, I'm afraid, Mrs. LaMer," the woman at the Early Education Service said, a little too sweetly, tapping Free's folder with her inch-long blue fingernails.

"You mean you're not quite ready for him," my mother said, just as sweetly, reaching over to tap the folder with her own short, unpainted fingernails. She hates it when people call her "Mrs."

So Free went to a private school, but he had to have a doctor's letter before even they would take him.

"I don't know what's wrong with him," Doctor Dan had said, "so what am I supposed to write in a letter?"

"There's *nothing* wrong with him," Mom said, "and you know it."

"Look, Annalise, Freeman is a very bright child, even gifted, but he's five years old and he is not verbal. That's not normal," Doctor Dan said. "I know you don't want to, but perhaps it's time to see a specialist." He reached for a pad. My mother got there first and pushed it out of his reach.

"Normal?" Mom's voice went up a notch. "He reads at the fifth-grade level, and he plays chess better than most adults. That's not normal either! Why don't those things bother you?"

"There are reasons for selective mutism," Doctor Dan said. "None of them are good: autism, schizophrenia, trauma—"

"I bet I've read more about selective mutism than you have," Mom said. "He's clearly not autistic, he hears fine, he shows no symptoms of schizophrenia, and the only trauma he experiences is people insisting he should talk!"

Doctor Dan closed his eyes and rested his forehead in one hand. I felt a little sorry for him.

"Why must there be a label or a syndrome for every aspect of life? He's just different." Mom turned Free's shirt right side out and started to pull it down over his head. "I like different. Different is good."

My brother's knee knocked mine, and when I looked up, Free was smiling at me. It was a small smile, the one that says, "Way to go, Mom!"

Mom hardly ever gets angry, at least with us, but that day I could see that she was afraid she might boil over and ruin Free's chances at kindergarten by not getting that letter. I knew how she felt, because sometimes I feel like I've swallowed a tightly wound spring that's going to cut loose—*boing!*—any minute. If it did, I would start whirling and never stop, round and round, bouncing off walls forever. If I could loosen that spring somehow, just gain a little slack, then I could coast for a long, long time.

Free knew how my mom felt too. He went over, put his hand on Doctor Dan's knee, and looked him in the eye. I know that face. Even people who can deal with my mom are no match for my brother. Doctor Dan looked at my mother, then at me. I sent him thoughts as hard as I could. *Just write the stupid letter.* Doctor Dan looked back at Free and sighed.

"Okay, have it your way. The letter will state that he's perfectly healthy and there is no known etiology for his delayed speech."

Mom let go a small sigh.

"But, Annalise, you're going to have to deal with this sooner rather than later. The world will bend for a silent five-year-old, but each year from here on out it will bend a little less."

"He'll talk when he's ready," Mom said. "He'll be just fine."

Outside Doctor Dan's, we did a three-way high five.

My mom isn't much taller than I am, but she looks taller because she is so slender and muscular. She used to take us on camping trips and for long bike rides, and she taught us both how to ski and swim. When I was little, I used to tell my mother she was beautiful, but she only laughed.

"All little girls think their mothers are beautiful," she would say, and then she would kiss me. "And all mothers know their little girls are beautiful, so it works out fine."

Her jeans are only a couple sizes bigger than mine, and the thin lines of gray in her light brown hair are the only way you can tell she isn't just my older sister. When I suggest that she dye it, she just gives me one of her that's-too-tacky-for-words looks.

"I didn't have gray hair before I had children," she'll say, raising an eyebrow. She always raises that eyebrow when she's thinking something she's too polite to say. I don't even think she knows that she does it. "I'm keeping my gray hair. I've earned every strand."

My mom is really weird sometimes.

Chapter 2

Have you ever thought that if one thing hadn't happened, a whole set of things never would have either? Like dominoes in time, a single event kicked off an unstoppable series of changes that gained momentum and spun out of control, and nothing was ever the same again. Don't ever doubt that a mere second can change your life forever.

On a Friday about a month and a half before school was out for the summer, my mom left work early to buy groceries before picking my brother and me up at the after-school program we both went to. She never liked shopping with us, and avoided it whenever she could, because she said it took twice as much time and three times as much money. If I hadn't pestered her for homemade pizza, if she hadn't said, "Hey, why not, it's Friday," she never would have gone to the supermarket to buy a crust mix, pizza sauce, pepperoni, and lots and lots of mozzarella cheese, never would have pulled out onto the highway when the light turned green, only to be hit in the driver's side by some guy who was too important to stop for a common red light. A couple of seconds one way and she would have come home grumbling about how this idiot had come from nowhere and forced her to slam on her brakes, a few seconds the other way and he would have been long gone before she stepped on the gas. Or maybe he would have crashed into some other poor kid's mom. For want of a pepperoni pizza, my life, as I knew it then, was lost.

At first it was cool when all the other kids started leaving before us. Often we were the first to be picked up, which was fine at the beginning of the year, because I didn't know anyone really, and I was one of the oldest kids there, on top of it. But since January, Elizabeth from my class at school had started coming three days a week, and we'd started to be friends, although she hadn't paid any attention to me before that. Actually, not many kids had paid much attention to me. The good kind of attention anyway. Elizabeth even introduced me to her best friend, Rachel, and the three of us had started hanging out, going to a movie now and then, or going to the mall, like real buddies.

When we first moved last year, I hated my new school so much that I told my mom I wasn't going anymore.

"You have to finish school so you can go to a good college," Mom said.

"What if I don't want to go to college at all?"

"You have to go to college so you can get a good job and support yourself."

"Maybe I'll just let my husband support me."

Mom raised her eyebrow at me.

"If that's what you decide after you have a good education and a good job, fine, but you will learn to support yourself."

"Then I want to be homeschooled!"

"Silly! I can't homeschool you, because I went to a good college and have a good job so I can support us."

Elizabeth's mother picked her up first, and then the other kids starting clearing out. Pretty soon Free and I had the computers all to ourselves without the usual time limits. We both got involved in what we were doing and didn't really notice we were the only ones left, until some lights started flicking off. Shirley was watching us, and she made an attempt to be cheery, but you could tell she was getting annoyed.

"Guess your mom had a meeting that went a little long, huh, guys?"

Free and I looked at each other. Mom was never late. We knew that. Shirley knew that.

We both went back to our games, but I could tell that Free wasn't really into it anymore, and neither was I. It was still light out, but you could tell the sun was starting to angle low.

Shirley left the room and I could see her pacing out in the hall, looking at her watch, cell phone at her ear. When she came back, she said, "Does your dad live close by?"

"No," I said. Maybe he did. I didn't know.

"Grandparents?"

"Don't have any."

Shirley sighed, then walked out of the room again. I could hear her shoes clicking in the hallway as she paced with her phone.

"Okay, guys, fifteen more minutes and then we're leaving. I've got a class tonight, and I can't hang around any longer."

"Where are we going?"

"Your mom listed your neighbor Penny as a contact. She'll meet us at your house."

Both of us had stopped playing on the computer.

"What if our mom shows up after we leave?" I asked.

"I'll leave a note for her."

Fifteen minutes went by and Mom didn't come. Shirley took us home, nobody saying anything. Of course, Free never does anyway. Penny was sitting on the porch step with our house key, and there was a sound like far-off thunder from inside the house.

"Babe is a little upset," Penny said. "He knows I'm out here, but there was no way I was going in without you."

"He wouldn't hurt you," I said.

"I wasn't concerned about him *hurting* me." Penny stood up and opened the door. Shirley's face did this classic horror movie expression—eyebrows up, mouth in an *O*—as she braced herself on the railing.

Babe knew enough not to blast through the doorway, but he did everything except that. Babe is a major beast, black and a hundred and fifty pounds, at least half of which my mom says is drool. Babe is a

Newfoundland, and sweet as syrup, but a little intense. We were late, and he knew it. He slimed us all as we entered, including Shirley, who was still a little in shock. She looked at the wide wet stripe Babe had laid up the side of her nice black pants. She went to rub it off, thought better of it, and stood there with her hands in the air.

"It sparkles when it dries," I said. I was trying to be helpful. Really.

Free grabbed Babe by the collar and tugged him away from Shirley. Of course, he couldn't have done it if Babe hadn't wanted to cooperate, but Babe generally tries to accommodate you once he gets the drift of what you want. Shirley left, still shooting glances at the viscous goo on her pants.

Penny lived alone next door, her husband dead, her kids grown and gone. She and my mom had struck up an odd friendship: Single Career Supermom meets Old-Fashioned Housewife. But like my mom says, if it ain't broke, don't fix it.

"Well," Penny said, with one of those looks of fake good cheer. I don't know who adults think they're fooling. "I'm sure your mom will be home soon. Probably a flat tire or something."

No way, Free and I both knew that. Mom hated cell phones, but flat tires were one of the reasons she carried one. If she wasn't answering her cell phone, there was a reason.

"Do you have any homework to do while I make something for you to eat?"

We shook our heads.

"Okay," she said, smile too wide. "I'll just see what I can find to feed you."

We were eating turkey sandwiches when there was a knock on the door. Free and I looked at each other and we knew. Penny took a little longer to catch on, but she toppled onto it as well when she opened the door and saw a guy in a uniform standing there. Blue uniform. Shiny badge. Crisp billed hat, which he took off when she answered the door.

"Oh, no," Penny said, then put her hand to her mouth. She stepped outside and shut the door behind her. I opened it again. The cop stopped in midsentence when he saw me—"emergency room" was all we heard. Free grabbed my hand and I held on tight. Penny turned to us, and we could see that her eyes were already that funny watery red that adults' eyes go when they try not to cry.

"Excuse me," she said, and walked into the house. I felt bad for the guy as he watched her leave. He took a deep breath and said one word: "Your-mom's-been-in-an-accident-but-she's-going-to-be-okay."

'Okay.' What precisely does that mean? I wondered. People were always saying things were going to be okay, but they never said when. Penny was crying because my mom was going to be okay? I didn't think so.

"Take us to her," I said. Free crowded in closer to me.

"She can't see you right now."

"I don't care if she can see us. We want to see her." Was she blind? I wondered.

Penny came up behind us, blowing her nose.

"Sorry," she said. "I just needed a minute."

"We want to see our mom," I said again, and Penny's and the policeman's eyes met above us. I hate it when adults do that.

The cop squatted down so he was at Free's eye level. I hate it when adults do that, too.

"She's in surgery. She may be there for a while."

"I don't care," I said, in what Mom calls my princess-wants-it-now voice.

Penny looked at the policeman. He looked at her.

"I'll call the hospital and find out when we can see her," she said.

Free and I looked at Penny.

"Why don't I go do that right now," she said, and walked back into the house.

The policeman put his hat on and left, his relief apparent.

Free and I sat on the step and watched the cop car drive off. I guess neither of us wanted to hear only Penny's end of the conversation with the hospital, for fear of what she might say.

After a while we heard steps from inside the house. The door opened.

"Well," Penny said in an everything's-going-to-be-just-fine voice, "she's still in surgery, but they will call us when she gets out. They said she won't come out of the recovery room until late tonight, and they suggested we come first thing in the morning. I'm sure that's what your mother would want. Okay?"

That "Okay?" got to me. Mom always says that no one, particularly adults speaking to children, should ever end a thought with "okay?" unless they really were asking for permission. Well, Penny wasn't getting my permission.

Free's lip started to quiver, but I squeezed his hand and just nodded at Penny. We sat at the table in front of our turkey sandwiches, none of us talking, none of us eating.

"I guess I'll go do some homework," I said to Penny. She nodded, not remembering I'd already told her I didn't have any. I knew she wanted to do something for us but didn't know what it could possibly be. Sometimes you just have to do things for yourself.

When Penny looked away, I beckoned for Free. He followed me, and I pulled him into my room.

"How much money do you have?" I whispered.

Without a fuss he got his bank, and we pooled our savings. I looked up taxis in the yellow pages and chose On-the-Double because I liked the name. I called and, using my best grown-up voice, inquired what the fare to the city hospital was, then asked to be picked up immediately. Free and I climbed out my window, glad that Babe was in the house instead of in the backyard, because he never would have let us sneak off. We walked a few houses down to the address I'd given On-the-Double, and when the taxi pulled up, we climbed in the back. The driver turned around and looked at us.

"Are we waiting for your mom or for your dad?"

"Neither," I said. "Our mother's been in a car accident, and we need to get to the hospital. We have enough money. I made sure before I called," I added, looking earnest and honest.

I wished he would get a move on. If Penny came out of the house, it was all over.

"Please hurry," I said, and I was surprised that my voice shook, even though I was acting.

"Anybody know you're going?" he asked.

"Yes, the neighbor, but she couldn't, um, accompany us. The hospital is expecting us."

At that, the taxi driver pulled away from the curb. He said nothing all the way to the hospital, but he kept glancing in his rearview mirror at us. When he let us out, I counted the exact fare out into his hand, mostly quarters and dimes, and Free and I ran into the hospital.

We followed the signs to the information desk, and I announced that we were there to see Annalise LaMer. A nurse, whose name tag said INGRID, glanced at me and then at Free.

"Is there an adult with you?"

"She *is* our adult."

Ingrid typed something into the computer. Then she summoned another nurse and they put their heads together, whispering. Ingrid made a phone call that I couldn't quite hear, but soon some guy in those weird green baggy hospital clothes came through the double doors and went over to the nurses. They gestured toward Free and me, then the three of them turned to huddle with their backs to us. The man finally walked toward us.

"Hey, guys, how's it going?"

I wanted to tell him not to bother with the buddy act, but I gave him my company best manners instead. Mom says you can think whatever you wish, but it's what you say and how you say it that will determine whether or not you get what you want.

"We're here to see our mother."

"I'm Dr. Racine. I saw your mom in the emergency room." My mother hates it when people introduce themselves with a title. "'Doctor' is a funny first name, don't you think?" she'd say. This probably wasn't the time to bring that up, though.

"How about if we get you guys a snack and—"

"We just want to see our mother, please."

"Who brought you here?"

"A taxi." Although that was a what, not a who.

"Where's your dad?"

"He's not around."

He squinted at me.

"At all," I said. This guy was a little slow for a doctor, I thought. Why are people so obsessed with someone who doesn't matter?

"How old are you?"

"Why?"

"There's a minimum age for the recovery room." He did his best to look sorry. I switched to my more assertive mode, the way I'd seen my mother do a number of times.

"We need to see our mother. Just for a few minutes, but we do need to see her. And we're not leaving until we do."

He exhaled a little. "Children aren't really allowed in the recovery room."

What did he mean by "really"? Were children "sort of" allowed in the recovery room?

"That's not a very kid-friendly policy," I said, then remembered my strategy and tried another tack. "Please. We haven't seen her since this morning. She didn't pick us up after school, and we didn't know

anything until a cop came and told us what happened. We came here as soon as we could. To. See.
Our. Mom."

The Racine guy smiled. I didn't see anything to
smile about.

"After surgery your mom will be very sleepy.
She'll be hooked up to some tubes and won't be able
to talk to you. I know for a fact that she's pretty
bruised up. She wouldn't want you to see her that
way, would she now? She wouldn't want you to be
frightened."

"We're already frightened." Duh.

The Racine guy stopped smiling. Ingrid came over
with some donuts and soda for us. That was not a
good sign—I have never seen a nurse sugar kids up.
She whispered something to the Racine guy, then gave
him a look that must have meant something to him.

"Okay," he said, after looking at his watch. "You
win. After they move your mom to the recovery room,
you can see her for five minutes. Five minutes. Only."

Free and I nodded.

"I'll come get you then," he said.

Ingrid gave Free and me each some crayons and a
coloring book, and we sat in the waiting room for

what seemed like a few days, not even pretending to color. We pretended to watch TV, pretended to look at magazines, and I pretended that I was not more terrified than I had ever been before in my life. It was solid black outside when the Racine guy came and got us. We followed him down a confusing series of halls, turning one way and then another, until we entered a room that was basically dark, with a few small, really bright lights.

"You can't touch her, okay?" There it was again: *Okay?* "Five minutes, and then you have to leave."

Free's fingernails dug into my hand so hard I almost pulled it away from him, but it was good to have something to focus on.

"The air bag broke her nose," the Racine guy said, "so she has black eyes. Her left arm, collarbone, and a couple of ribs are broken as well."

That didn't sound too terrible. "Is she going to be okay?"

He paused. "Her hip bone was pretty cracked up, as well as her thigh and left knee. It all had to be pinned and screwed together."

I thought of the screwdriver Mom had used to put up our basketball hoop. I thought of safety pins.

I thought doctors were supposed to use sophisticated implements, not carpenter's tools.

At first I didn't recognize the woman lying on the table. Her face was a mess, all swollen and bruised. My mom never stopped moving, but this person was very, very still. It was my mom's hair, though. Long and thick like mine. Light brown, a little wavy. A few strands of gray.

A nurse was by Mom's side, adjusting some tube. She looked up at us, and then glanced at the doctor.

"Her children," the Racine guy said. He seemed to be apologizing. "I told them only five minutes."

"She may look bad, but she's not in any pain," the nurse said. "She's going to be okay, but your mom is going to have a long road ahead of her. You're going to have to help her get better, all right?"

I reached out and squeezed Mom's hand when the nurse turned her back. Mom told me once that some rules are made to be broken. The Racine guy started to say something, then stopped.

"Everything's going to be fine, Mom," I said.

"She can't hear you, sweetie," the nurse said, her back still to us.

"Yes, she can," I said, for Mom had squeezed my hand back. A single tear ran down the side of her face and Free reached up to wipe it. Then he put his hand over both of ours, and I swear my mom smiled.

"Right now she needs all her energy to get better," the Racine guy said. "You can come back in the morning and see her again."

When we got back to the waiting room, the taxi man was there. So was Penny. I could see she was torn between feeling bad for us and bawling us out.

The taxi man stepped forward.

"Sorry, guys," he said. "It just didn't feel quite right. After I got off work, I went back to where I picked you up and started knocking on doors. This woman was beside herself looking for you. She even called the cops." Penny looked at us and took a deep breath, in preparation for some sort of lecture.

"Thank you," I said to him, and then to Penny before she could say anything, "We're ready to go now."

Actually, I was glad they were there. I hadn't thought about getting back home, and we didn't have enough money for another taxi.

The taxi guy looked at us, then gave both Penny and me his card.

"Call me if I can help," he said. Then he handed back the pile of change I had given him. "No charge for emergencies," he said.

Chapter 3

When the three of us went back in the morning, Mom was in a regular hospital room. Her face was even more swollen and purple than it had been the night before.

"Oh, Annalise!" Penny gasped. She went to the bedside, gripped my mom's right hand, and promptly started crying. So there's my mom, all banged up, broken, black and blue, and Penny is the one who's crying. My mom patted Penny's hand gently, then reached out her hand to Free and me.

"Thanks for coming to see me last night." Her words were a little burbled through her fat lips. "You guys were all I could think about after it happened. You would be stuck at school forever, wondering where I was." She smiled a little, but with her face so swollen it looked more like she was stretching some kind of awful Halloween mask. "You didn't get that pizza after all."

"We'll make pizza when you come home," I said.

"We'll have to go back to the store first," she said. "When I saw the pizza sauce on the windshield, I thought it was blood." She started to chuckle, then stopped and reached for her ribs. "I didn't bleed much, but I sure broke, didn't I?"

A nurse came in with a syringe. "Your mom needs her meds now. She'll be out of commission for a while, so why don't you guys scoot down to the cafeteria. You can come back later."

With a little wave my mom closed her eyes, and we left.

Penny took us to see Mom on Sunday, too, and we talked her into letting us skip school on Monday so we could stay with her all day again. Free and I sat for hours in Mom's room, playing chess and cards, sometimes watching TV on low. The nurses kept us fed, and clucked a lot. Most of the time Mom was asleep, or drugged, but when she was awake, she would just watch us, hardly saying anything. I had never seen her in bed for so long. I had also never seen anyone so ugly before, and her face got worse before it got better.

It was scary without Mom at home, even though Penny stayed with us. Free took to hiding in closets and sucking his thumb again. He crawled into my bed at night, and even though I tried to comfort him, I was very glad to feel him warm and close. My mother had always been invincible, and now I realized that she, too, like my father, could disappear forever. Free had never known our dad, so this was a first for him.

Mom told us we had to go to school on Tuesday. I thought we should have gotten at least a week off, but she was firm.

"We've played around enough," she said. "Now I have work to do."

I knew what she meant. I'd seen them help her sit up, watched her bite her lip as they flexed her left leg.

"Penny, do you know anyone I could pay to deal with things until I get out of here?" Mom asked.

Penny looked at her in disgust.

"I'll stay with Free and Lise until you get out," she said. "I can't believe you'd think otherwise."

"I'd appreciate it if you would stay with them at night, because they're comfortable with you, but they'll need someone to shop and cook for them, and—I hate to say it—the house is a disaster. I won't have you cleaning."

Penny opened her mouth.

"Don't argue," Mom said. "It's not negotiable." *Not negotiable* is what Mom says when she's really serious. Most things with her are negotiable, but when she says they aren't, she means it.

They ended up agreeing that Penny would stay overnight and get us off to school in the morning, but that she would hire someone for the rest of the stuff.

We had never had hired help before, even though Mom had always worked. Correction: always worked "outside the home," because Mom says that by definition *all* mothers work. Mom also says that everyone needs to clean up their own messes, so whenever she told us to, we hauled out the vacuum and a dust cloth, a mop, and a bucket. She would put on loud, fast music, and we'd all dance as we sucked up the dog hair and dust bunnies and scrubbed the first layer of dog tracks off the kitchen floor. My mom played a mean air guitar. Free was a hot dancer for a five-year-old, and Babe howled with great feeling.

It was upsetting having other people in our house. Penny was okay, but Mrs. Biggens, the woman she found to shop, cook, and clean, wasn't. Mrs. Biggens may have been only part-time help, but she was a full-time witch. She was large in a really scary sort of way, with odd mustard-yellow hair whose color and fluffy shape couldn't possibly be real. Her normal hair must have been really bad if she thought this wig was an improvement. Mrs. Biggens wore a lot of makeup, but even that didn't cover up a pretty serious mustache, and she must not have had a mirror at her house, because it looked like most of the makeup she put on had missed its target. On top of all that, she smelled like something that had died. Once I saw her pull a bottle of perfume from her purse and spritz it on herself—she had actually *paid* for something that smelled that bad! We probably could have handled all that if she had been a nice person, but she wasn't. Free and I despised Mrs. Biggens. I called her BigBuns, because they were, and to make Free smile.

BigBuns said she was allergic to animals and made Babe stay outside when she was with us, but I think she just didn't like Babe. If she'd really been allergic, she would have been miserable from all the dog dander *inside* the house. After we ate up all the casseroles and goodies that people from my mom's office had brought over, we almost starved. Well, not really, but it seemed like it. I was pretty sure BigBuns kept most of the grocery money that Penny gave her, because she fed Free and me cold sandwiches or canned soup every night. I saw some good stuff in the grocery bags that BigBuns carried in, but Free and I never got any of it. When I told Penny these things, I could tell she didn't want or didn't know how to deal with it. It made me angry, because on top of not cooking, BigBuns didn't clean much either. Whenever I tried to stand up to her about something, she got nasty.

"I just don't know how your poor mother manages with such disobedient children!" or "If I was your mom, I'd stay in the hospital as long as I could too."

Mom came home after about two weeks, and only then because she pitched a hissy fit, saying hospitals were hardly a place to get better. The doctors finally gave in and she called our taxi man, whose name was Gray, to bring her home. He lifted her into the car, then put her wheelchair in the trunk, and unloaded them both when he got to our house.

"Like a sack of potatoes," Mom said, grimacing.

"Prettiest sack of potatoes in the world," Gray said, as he placed her back in the wheelchair as carefully as my mom handled my grandmother's good dishes at our holiday meals.

I thought my mom would say something snotty and short to him, but she surprised me.

"You are a very sweet man," she said, patting his arm.

That made me look at Gray a little more closely. He must have been old enough to be my great-grandfather, with a pruny face and scruffy gray-black whiskers. Some pretty good-looking guys had taken my mom out, and she'd never called any of them sweet. Quite the contrary.

Things got a little better after Mom came home. It was a relief just to be able to go look at her whenever we wanted, even if she still slept most of the time. When she was awake, Mom spent a lot of time on the telephone, and I heard the words "disability" and "insurance" a lot. Penny stayed with us only occasionally now, but BigBuns was still very much around. At least when my mother was awake, BigBuns pretended to do some cleaning, and she actually put hot food that didn't come from a can on the table before she left. A nurse came to our house every day, as well as a physical therapist. Mom still had to go to doctor appointments, and Gray always took her and brought her back. We settled into a strange routine, but at least it was a routine.

The afternoon my mother went to get her arm cast off, BigBuns was in a truly bad mood, even for her. A storm had been blowing up all day, and it seemed that the darker it got outside the house, the blacker her mood got inside the house.

I jumped when the phone rang. I guess I was a little nervous since the accident. It was Mom calling to say that the clinic was running late due to delays, and she asked to talk to BigBuns. Even Mom called her that.

"Certainly," BigBuns said into the telephone. "I'd be happy to stay." Then she slammed the handset down and glared at Free and me. "The nerve!"

There was a streak of lightning in the window, and the sky rumbled. Outside in his pen, Babe howled.

For dinner BigBuns slapped sandwiches down on paper plates and set an open bag of potato chips on the table. I poured milk for Free and me, but it was sour. Free raised his sandwich to his lips and then threw it down. It was peanut butter and jelly. We never have peanut butter and jelly sandwiches.

"Free can't eat that!" I said.

"He can eat it or not eat it, but this is dinner."

I knew Free was hungry. I had seen the tuna sandwich still wrapped up in his school lunch box.

It smelled worse than mine had, even through the plastic. He sat at the table with his eyes closed, and two tears bubbled up in the corners of his eyes.

"It's okay, Free. I'll fix you something else," I said.

"There is nothing else. Hush up and eat your sandwiches, both of you," BigBuns said.

I'd seen some frozen entrées around a day or so ago. I knew I hadn't eaten them. I tried to reason with her.

"He can't eat peanut butter," I said. "The first time he did, he threw up and got these bright red splotches all over. He couldn't stop scratching and we had to take him to the emergency room."

"I don't believe it. Eat those sandwiches."

Not being verbal had never hindered Free's ability to communicate. He peeled his sandwich apart and threw half of it at BigBuns. For a five-year-old he has a good arm. And a good aim. The bread hit BigBuns on the nose, then hung a split second before sliding sluglike off her chin, leaving a sticky purple and brown trail. She reached a hand up to her face, then picked the oozing piece of bread off her chest where it had landed.

"That does it!" she yelled, advancing on Free. I'd

never seen an adult so angry. I wasn't sure what to do. I'd only ever had to protect Free from little kids' mean words before.

"*What is going on?*"

The three of us stopped and turned. My mother was in the doorway, Gray pushing her wheelchair. Her hair was wild from the wind and rain, but it was nothing compared to her eyes.

"She's making Free eat pbj's!"

"My son is allergic to peanuts, and if he were a less sensible child, you would be calling an ambulance by now. Or Lise would. And why is our dog outside in the rain?"

"She always makes us keep Babe outside when you're not here," I said, wondering what evil BigBuns would inflict on me the next time I was alone with her.

"Go away," Mom said to BigBuns. "Now. And do not come back."

Mom was gritting her teeth. If she hadn't been in the wheelchair, I would have felt sorry for BigBuns. No, probably not.

"You owe me six hours' pay," BigBuns said. "Two of it overtime."

"And you owe my children an apology. You pay up first, and then I will."

"I see where your children get their contrariness."

"I'm glad you see the resemblance."

BigBuns harrumphed and stamped and started to argue, but Gray stepped in front of my mother.

"You heard her. You can apologize and leave, or you can just leave," he said. BigBuns sputtered some more, but the important thing was that she left, and fast, with traces of grape jam like some kind of misplaced makeup still on her face. When BigBuns was out the door, Mom sagged into the wheelchair. She looked more tired than I had ever seen her, and something else—a little . . . old? My mother had never looked old to me before.

"Gray, hand me the telephone, please. What do you guys want on your pizza?"

"Anchovies!" I said.

"Whenever you ask for anchovies, you eat half of one and pick the rest off," Mom said.

"I think I like them now." I liked the idea of liking anchovies, at least.

So we had a party. Gray brought a very wet and agitated Babe into the house, and we put on music and ate two large pizzas, but we all picked off the anchovies. Mom let us drink all the soda we wanted, and Free and I got a little giddy knowing BigBuns wasn't coming back. It was a little foolish not to realize that other arrangements would need to be made.

Free and I went grocery shopping with Gray the next day. We brought home bags and bags of groceries loaded with all sorts of good stuff. The three of us hauled them in and put everything away. Gray refused the money my mother offered him for his help.

"Annalise, you got enough troubles. It's the least I can do."

I wasn't sure I liked this guy calling my mother by her first name, but she didn't seem to mind.

With Mom's instructions, Free sorted laundry and ran the washing machine. I loaded the dishwasher and helped with Free's bath, taking a glass of water to my mother so she could test the temperature before he got in. He even let me wash his hair. We tried to do some vacuuming and dusting, but it wasn't any fun without Mom. Mom wasn't sleeping as much now, and she read aloud to us every night. We found all the restaurants in our area that delivered, and it was good to feel like we were back to not needing anybody again.

One night about a week after BigBuns left, we were eating the dinner I'd made, consisting of a box of macaroni and cheese and a salad of some early lettuce from Penny's garden. Free had made the salad, actually. He had a great time cutting the lettuce into identically sized squares with a pair of scissors.

"We're going on a vacation," Mom said.

Free and I looked at her, then at each other. Vacations were for hiking, or skiing, or biking. She couldn't even walk—how could we go on a vacation?

"I'm on medical leave from work and you guys are getting out of school soon. In a few days I'll start using a walker, and I need a change of scenery. We all need a change of scenery. We're going to a beach."

"A beach vacation?" We'd never had one of those before. I'd never even seen the ocean for real.

"An island, actually," Mom said. "It's pretty much all beach."

Wow. An island vacation. I thought of an ad I'd seen for a Hawaiian luxury resort, and I could see us in grass skirts, drinking from coconuts.

"Where?"

"Fiddle Beach. In Maine, where I grew up."

We had never been to Maine. I knew Mom had grown up there, the "only child of only children," as she liked to say. I knew too that she had moved away to go to college and had never gone back after her parents died a few years later. But that's all I knew.

"For how long?" I asked.

"For the rest of the summer!" Mom said. "Isn't that great?"

No, it wasn't great. Free and I looked at each other again, the Mom-has-lost-it look.

"What about my camps?" I'd picked out two this summer, rock climbing and art camp. For once I wouldn't be going alone: I'd be with Elizabeth at one, with Rachel at the other. We were going to perform daring technical maneuvers on sheer rock faces and create stunning masterpieces together. It was all planned.

"Fiddle Beach is better than any camp," Mom replied. It was more the look on her face than her words that stopped me from asking anything more.

Chapter 4

Under Mom's supervision, Free and I packed a suitcase each and a few boxes with games and supplies.

"Don't need much beyond a bathing suit," she said. "I've rented a furnished house, right down to the pots and pans."

I tried to bring a box of books, but Mom said there wouldn't be enough room in the car.

"Not to worry," she said. "The library is within walking distance."

I couldn't believe Gray agreed to drive us all the way to Maine in his taxi, Babe and all. Penny was there to see us off, fussing over all of us like usual. I could see she thought Mom was nuts, and I was glad someone agreed with me.

"How are you going to manage up there, Annalise? You don't have a car, and you couldn't drive one even if you did. You can hardly even stand up."

My mom held out our house key. "You take care of my plants, Penny, and I'll take care of us. It will be great. It's just what I need. The sea cures everything."

Whenever we'd had long drives before, Mom had played Ghost with us, or we had sung "99 Bottles of Beer on the Wall," or listened to a book on tape, but this time my mom and Gray sat in the front seat and she pretty much ignored us. Seems he'd been in the navy when he was younger, and loved the ocean. Seems he actually knew someone from Maine who knew my grandfather. Blah blah blah.

Free and I nearly suffocated. The suitcases took up all the trunk space, so the boxes went under our feet, and we had to balance Free's piano keyboard across our laps. Babe alone took up more than half of the backseat. He drooled even more when he was excited, and pretty soon I felt not only left out but damp. There wasn't anything else to do, so Free, Babe, and I all fell asleep.

I smelled it before I heard it. I woke up, sniffed, inhaled more deeply, then again. We had been on the highway when I fell asleep, but were now on a smaller road in what looked to be a very tiny town. Free struggled to sit up, sniffing as well, his sleep horns making him look demonic. My mother turned and looked at us, said nothing, then turned back around, smiling. I noticed she was taking deep breaths too.

"Sweet saline rot," she said.

"It's a fine smell, it is," Gray said.

Mom pointed. "Turn right at that corner. The road leads out to the island. Used to be the only way onto Fiddle Beach unless you took a boat, but I hear they've put in some kind of breakwater now." We drove down a road that looked like it had nothing but mucky, soggy sand on either side of it.

"What's wrong with the land?" I asked.

"Tide's on the ebb," she said. As if I knew what that meant.

Pretty soon the land got normal again. More normal, I should have said. I'd figured out there wouldn't be tiki huts in Maine, but I had expected a few luxury hotels at least. Instead, the first building I saw had a huge fake lobster crawling on its roof. How tacky. Its claws hung over the front of the building and held a sign that read BLUE LOBSTER RESTAURANT. Next to the restaurant was a poor, dilapidated shack that looked like the paint had been scraped off it.

Over the door was a plastic piece of driftwood with THE BEACH BUM lettered on it. Across the street was a funny flat-roofed building with four open garage doors on the front. At first I thought it was completely dark inside the garage doors, but then I caught a glimpse of some strange flashing lights.

"That arcade's new," Mom said. "Used to be a creamee stand there."

Next to the arcade was an odd construction that seemed to be made entirely of fishing nets and weird bowling-pin-shaped things. THE FISH MARKET, the lettering on the window said. How original.

"At least the Fish Market hasn't changed a bit," Mom said. "Probably even the same nets and floats from when I lived here."

Next to the Fish Market was a house, and then another house, and then another. I guessed we had concluded our tour of downtown Fiddle Island.

And then I heard it. A rush of water, whooshing and gushing, crashing and spraying. It made me want to pee.

And then I saw it. The land just ended, chop, and an enormous flat empty grayness stretched beyond it forever. There was nothing to see except water, and then more water. I'd never seen anything so depressing. No wonder people used to think ships might fall off the edge of the world.

The more I looked at the ocean, trying to take it in, the more I got taken in by it instead. All that space, so immense and immeasurable. I got that scary, shaky feeling I get when I lie on my back at night and stare up at the starry night sky. Infinite. It was a word that I couldn't get my head around. Endless. I shivered. You don't want to start thinking that way, because you might not be able to stop.

The road followed the shape of the island, and as we drove we saw some pretty nice houses. *This might not be so bad,* I started thinking. A house on the beach with a spiral staircase, skylights, maybe a cupola I could have all to myself . . . but we drove by them all until it looked as if there weren't any more houses left before the beach ended in a funny high wall of rocks—except one.

It was when I saw the house that I knew Mom had really lost it. It was more of a shack really, small, with a front porch that slanted a little to one side. No spiral staircase. No cupola. No skylights. There was hardly even any paint left on the outside of it, but my mother acted as if it were a four-star resort.

"Beachfront property!" She chortled. "I can't believe how lucky we were to get it on such short notice. And so inexpensively!" She saw my face. "Hey, Lise! It's got the only three things we need. Location, location, location." Mom pointed at the wall of rocks that ran from the mainland across to the island. Built of boulders as tall as I and at least twenty feet high, that wall wasn't put there by Mother Nature. "Although that breakwater does ruin the view a little bit."

I thought of the house we'd built last year and how persnickety my mom had been, making sure everything was just so. From choosing the layout of the house to the landscaping, she had been specific and particular. Consequently, it was gorgeous. Everyone said so. She had let me decorate my own room and didn't fuss a bit when I chose purple and red for my color scheme. It was a beautiful bedroom, with strands of clear Christmas lights and a computer with my own line to the Internet. Maybe my room was partly why Elizabeth and Rachel had decided I couldn't be so bad after all. We had such a nice house—so what were we doing here?

Mrs. Lafayette, who owned the house, came a few

minutes later. She eyed Gray's taxi, then my brother and me. She glared at Babe, who had gone berserk the minute he escaped the taxi. He was chasing waves, barking at them, snapping at the spray, then turning and running from them when they advanced on him.

"I told you I had a dog," Mom said, catching the look.

"Looks more like a horse," Mrs. Lafayette said.

"Who needs a horse, when you have a dog like that?" Gray said.

"And when will your husband be joining you?" Mrs. Lafayette said, taking the check Mom handed her.

"He won't," Mom said, and turned back to the water. For the first time I realized she probably got as tired as I did of accounting for that man's absence.

"I'm sorry, I didn't realize your family wasn't . . . intact."

"Oh, our family is quite intact," my mother said.

Mrs. Lafayette sighed. "So difficult without a man around the house."

"We manage somehow," Mom said, raising her right eyebrow. "That breakwater never used to be there. When was it built?"

"Must be eleven, twelve years ago now. Stupid place for a breakwater, if you ask me. Some idiots use it like a walking bridge from the mainland. But according to the folks who own the houses farther north on this side of the island, it's paid for itself already."

"And according to you?"

Mrs. Lafayette shrugged. "Any fool born here knows you don't put a fancy house where the sea can get it. It's just a matter of time before you have to pay more than you're willing."

"But your house has been here since I was a kid," Mom said.

Mrs. Lafayette looked at her. "It ain't fancy now, is it?"

I should say not.

Mrs. Lafayette probably would have stayed the entire afternoon, but it was clear to all of us from the way my mom stared out to sea that she wasn't listening to anyone. Mrs. Lafayette tried a few more topics and finally left.

"Take me to the beach, Gray," Mom commanded.

Gray wheeled her down to the beach, the wheelchair tires biting into the sand. Free and I followed.

Mom breathed deeply and closed her eyes.

"Listen to the rhythm," she said. "Listen to that." Then she opened her eyes and stared out over that bleak, watery wasteland.

"Come on, kids," Gray said. "Help me unload."

I looked at Mom to see if we had to, but she wasn't paying any attention to us. So Free and Gray and I hauled our few things into that ratty excuse for lodgings. Free and I were to share the loft, which was a third of the size of the purple and red room I had all to myself at home. The loft walls were pink, my least favorite color. It figured. None of the windows had curtains, and the kitchen didn't have cupboards, just some rough shelves. The single bathroom didn't even have a door. At home there was a bathroom for each of us, *with* doors. This was pathetic.

Afterward, when we went back down to where Mom sat at the water's edge, her eyes were still fixed in the distance. What she expected to see, I don't know.

"Could you bring me the walker, please, Gray?"

"I don't think that's a good idea, Annalise."

She looked at him with her Did-I-ask-you-what-you-thought? look.

"Can't tell that woman a damn thing," he muttered.

Free and I nudged each other. It wasn't the first time we had heard *that*.

With a disgusted look on his face, Gray trundled back to the house and returned with the walker, which he placed in front of Mom. The walker's legs poked into the sand, and it wobbled a little as Mom tried to raise herself up out of the wheelchair.

"Give me a boost, Lise," she said. I wasn't strong enough, and in the end Gray had to heft her up enough to lean against the walker. She swayed a little in place at first, then, concentrating hard, she pushed the walker ahead a few inches. She dragged her bad leg forward, then leaned most of her weight on the walker and took a short little step with her good leg. The suspense was worse than watching Free learn to walk.

"What if you fall, Annalise?"

"Then I'll just have to get up, won't I?"

After a few more steps, Gray grumbled, "All right, all right. You've had your fun. Now sit down before you fall down." Gray pushed the wheelchair behind my mom, and she sat down hard in it, wincing. She was sweating, but she looked very pleased.

"I learned to walk here once before, Gray. I can do it again."

Gray shook his head. "Give me your grocery list," was all he said, and when she did, he left.

"Look at all the garbage on the beach," Mom said, more to herself than anyone else. "There never used to be so much garbage. Of course, there never used to be so many houses. Or that atrocious breakwater." Then to us: "What are you waiting for? Put some sunscreen on each other and go play in the water. Just stay off the breakwater. Free's legs aren't long enough yet."

Free and I put our swimsuits on and took off toward the surf. The waves foamed as they hit the sand. We touched our toes in and then ran back to Mom, shrieking.

"It's freezing!" I said.

"Of course it's freezing! It's Maine. You'll get use to it." She smiled. "Actually, you'll just go numb. Just get out of the water if you feel shooting pains in your arms and legs. That's dangerous. Go back and jump in all at once. It's the best way. You'll love it!"

Free and I looked at each other. This was our mother who checked up on us every five minutes in six inches of bathwater. Free shook his head at me. I agreed.

Instead, we took pans and plastic bowls from the

shack down to the shore and made a sand castle, complete with shell borders and seaweed walkways. Breaking only for the sandwiches Gray brought back—there wasn't even any fast food available, can you believe that?—it took us the better part of the afternoon to finish our creation. Gray came to see us before he started the drive back. After admiring our handiwork, he gave Free and me each his card again.

"You call me if you need anything. Anytime. Collect. I told your mom the same thing, but she's a stubborn one. You take care of her now."

We nodded. Gray wheeled Mom to the horrible little house and carried her up the steps over her protests that she needed to learn to manage them on her own.

"So start tomorrow, okay?" Gray said.

When I looked back, she was reaching her hand up to pat his cheek. I turned away.

Free and I put a dinner of cold cuts on the table. Afterward we wanted Mom to see the sand castle, but she was too tired.

"I have an idea," she said. "Bring me the camera."

She put the telephoto lens on the camera and sent us down to pose by our creation. When we got there, however, it was clear that something was amiss. The water that had been a good thirty feet from the castle when we left it now licked perilously close to our fortress of sand. Free looked from the castle to the waves, then back again. Walking around in front of the castle, he held up his hand like a traffic cop. *Stop*, he meant.

When we got back to the house, Mom was in tears, her shoulders still heaving hard from laughing.

"My King Canute," she said, in broken gasps, "trying to stop the tide."

I didn't know who King Canute was, but it was good to hear her laugh. It had been a long time. Maybe she knew what she was doing after all.

Chapter 5

That night, trying to go to sleep in that wretched pink loft, I thought I would go crazy. The sound of the sea kept me awake; it surrounded me, never falling silent for a second, filling my ears and my mind. I must have finally drifted off, because I woke up thinking it was raining, a torrential rain in a vicious storm full of angry wind. When I looked out the window, though, the sky was clear, the moon was bright, and there was no wind at all. All I'd heard was the sound of waves, the ocean near our door. It still made me want to pee.

In the morning I had a horrible sunburn. Free and I had put on the same sunscreen and had been out the same length of time, but he had turned a lovely toasted-marshmallow amber. My skin was red and hot, and it hurt. It wasn't fair.

"It's just a sunburn, Lise," Mom said. "Deal with it."

Not an ounce of sympathy from someone I could usually count on to fuss over my slightest discomfort.

She put aloe on my burn and told me to wear a shirt when I wasn't in the water.

"You're at the beach! Swim! Play in the water! Enjoy it!" she said, shooing us out the door. Once outside, Free and I stopped and looked at each other. I don't think she had ever shooed us before.

At home Mom always called me her freshwater fish because she could never get me out of the swimming pool. I had bugged her to put in a pool at our real house, but she said it was safer that I went to the city pool, because if we had one at home, I would probably dissolve. As long as the water is clear and the bottom is concrete, I can swim and dive and do dead man's float in the water all day.

But the ocean—now there's another story.

I tried. I really did. I went out into the water up to my knees, even though the cold burned like fire. Then I made the mistake of looking down. I saw all this *stuff*—seaweed rolling and twisting, a few fish and a ghostly floating plastic bag that at first I thought was a jellyfish. I looked out at the miles and miles of nothing but water—moving, churning water—and I realized there could be anything out there, anything at all. Where I could see bottom, there might be a piece

of glass or a sharp shell hidden under the sand waiting to slice into my soft feet, and where I couldn't see
bottom, who knows? I thought of how people on the
surface must look to the sea creatures below, to
sharks in particular—fragile flippery arms and legs
beckoning *Eat me! Eat me!* like convenient snacks. And
there was always the pull, the pull of the tide that
sucked the sand from beneath you grain by grain, trying to suck you with it.

And then there was Babe. Newfoundlands are nat-
urally good water dogs, and they are often trained to
pull nets and rescue people, but Babe had never been
trained, so he only panicked when Free and I went in
the water. The first time he bounded into the water,
splashing and barking like a canine maniac, he
created a mini tidal wave. When he reached us, he
couldn't control his momentum and knocked us
both down in the icy water. We came up coughing
and yelling at him. So much for rescuing us.

Twice Free and I walked him back to the house
and tried to sneak back into the icy surf, stretching as
tall as we could on our tippy-toes to delay the rise of
the frigid water, but eventually Babe would look up
from his chew toy and decide we were in mortal

danger. The third time Mom had us tie him to the deck, where he still made noise, but at least he couldn't drown us.

Mom kept insisting that we play in the water.

"I grew up here," she said. "It's perfectly safe. Trust me, you'll get accustomed to the cold. In the summer I spent more of my day in the water than out."

We tried, but our skin raised in goose bumps and our eyes stung from the salt. When our lips turned blue, Free and I looked at each other and gave up. We were happier, Babe was happier, even if my mother wasn't. When I changed out of my swimsuit, a pile of sand, small shells, and pebbles laced with ferny seaweed fell out onto the floor. Ugh.

After we got dry clothes on, Free and I took the pots and pans again and a spade from the porch and built the biggest sand castle we could. The sand grated against my burn and worked itself into my soft spots, but we kept going. At last the castle walls were over four feet high, surrounded by massive trenches two feet deep. It was a glorious structure, better than yesterday's, with flags we made by gluing foil to Popsicle sticks. Free put little green plastic army men on the castle in strategic spots, and we pretended they were knights. When we went in for a late lunch, Mom gave me her camera to take a picture.

"Before it disappears," she said. One of Free's eyebrows went up, just like Mom's. "Remember yesterday?" she said to him. "How the tide knocked it down?"

"But we built it farther up on the beach this time," I said.

"No, you didn't. It just looked like that because the tide was out farther when you started."

I must have looked puzzled, because she continued, "The tide goes out twice a day, and it comes in twice a day. See that line of seaweed up there? Nothing on the beach up to that line will exist after high tide." Mom handed us something ripped from the newspaper Gray had bought. "This is the tide chart for the month. See? Low tide, high tide, low tide, high tide. Changes a little every day. You need to pay attention to the tides here to be safe."

"That's just one more point in favor of a swimming pool, as far as I'm concerned," I said.

"Just go take a picture of the castle before it gets washed away."

Free gave her his stubborn look.

"Come on," I said. "We'll show her."

Free and I went back out and began reinforcing the castle. We hauled rocks from wherever we could find them and ringed the moat with them, rolling the ones that were too heavy to lift. We lined them up, then chinked the holes with shells and gravel. For good measure we wrapped it all in long strips of seaweed that looked like brown overcooked lasagna noodles. I held one up to the back of my shorts.

"Look, Free! I have a dragon tail! No! I'm draggin' a tail. Get it?"

He giggled.

"No, wait! I have a dragon tale about draggin' a dragon tail!" We nearly fell over laughing.

Through that entire afternoon the tide advanced, inch by wet inch, until it licked at our fortress. We watched, confident that our engineering skills were more than a match for mere water, and indeed, the first wave that reached it did no damage at all. The moat took on water and I heard the rattle of small rocks settling, but when the water pulled back, our fort was strong, unharmed. Free and I high-fived each other.

It wasn't until about the sixth wave that things started to come undone. At first just a few of the smallest pebbles shook loose and tumbled toward the sea. When we scrambled to do maintenance, we got swamped by a large wave that took out all our repairs and then some.

An hour later nothing was left except a few rocks scattered on the beach.

"Wow," I said. Free nodded.

"Can't fight the tide," Mom said when we got back. I hate it when she's right.

The next day Free's skin was the color of melted marmalade cats, but my sunburn had a sunburn. It hurt to put on clothes, it hurt to go out in the sun. The sheer presence of sand on my skin was excruciating.

"This is not fair! I'm in agony!" I said to Mom.

She just shrugged. "Part of the territory. You'll either learn to cover up or wear sunscreen. Or suffer." First "deal with it," now "suffer." This was my mother talking?

While Mom rested, Free and I worked on a sand sculpture of a dragon (*really* high up on the beach this time). Babe watched intently in case we decided to do something life threatening, like wash our feet. After about an hour he stood and barked once, his signal that we were to pay attention. I turned and saw a boy and a girl approaching from the north beach. Only an occasional few made it down this far, or straggled over atop the breakwater from the mainland, and never kids by themselves. Usually jogging, puffing old men or a family out strolling. I'd said hi to a couple of kids with their parents before, but one look at our shack was enough for them to lose interest in me. Who cared? Snobs.

The boy was walking a bike, the girl was just walking. The boy was about my height, skinnier than even me, and was what Rachel would call butt-ugly. My mother would probably just say he was "homely." Big nose, buckteeth, pointy chin, eyes too close together, and lots of black hair. Glasses on top of all that, nerdy black plastic ones. Hadn't this guy ever seen any fashion magazines? The girl was taller, on the chunky side, and walked a little funny, her toes pointed in. As she approached, I could see from her face that she had Down syndrome and that she, too, wore glasses. Hers, however, were quite stylish.

The boy walked right up to us.

"My dad told me someone had moved into this old place. I didn't believe it."

"Believe it," I said. "It was a spur-of-the-moment kind of thing. All the good places were taken. Our real house is very nice." I paused. "Very *very* nice." It seemed important to make that quite clear.

"I'm Arthur," he said. It figured, he looked like an Arthur. Arthur is not a cool name. At least not for a kid. "This is my cousin. Her name is Beth."

"Hello, Beth," I said. "I'm Lise."

"Hi, Lise," Beth said. Her words weren't quite right. Arthur watched me the way I watched kids when I introduced Free.

"And this is Free," I said, gesturing to my brother, who had come to stand close beside me.

"Hi, Free," Arthur said.

Free nodded.

"Hi, Free," Beth said.

Free nodded again.

"He doesn't talk," I said. Arthur's eyebrows went up in interest.

"You know what I do to people who hassle him?" I asked, just so he wouldn't get ideas.

"What?"

"First I slug them really hard in the gut, then I push them down and sit on them. Sometimes I punch them in the face. Bloody noses make a real mess." Okay, I'd only done it once, but I had impressed myself.

Arthur nodded. He was impressed too.

"Cool," he said. "My dad's the town cop."

"Cool," I said.

"Beth has Down syndrome," he said.

"I can see that," I said.

Arthur's eyes narrowed and, for the first time, I realized I could be on the receiving, rather than the presenting, end of a bloody nose. "There's nothing wrong with her hearing. And at least she talks."

"I didn't mean anything."

He nodded at me. "Okay."

I couldn't think of anything else to say.

"I hate summer people," Arthur said after a moment.

"I'm a summer person," I said.

"No, you're not. Summer people live in the nice places. And we have to be polite to them because they spend so much money here."

"I bet they're the ones who leave all the garbage on the beach."

Arthur nodded. "And they treat us like servants."

Free handed Beth a bowl he'd been using to fashion

dragon scales. Free doesn't play with just anybody.

"So, welcome to Fiddle Beach," Arthur said.

"Why is it called Fiddle Beach?"

"The island is shaped like a fiddle, isn't it? Upside-down one. Fat, then skinny, then fat, then there's this bar like a fiddle neck that tapers off into nothing." Arthur pointed. "Just over that breakwater is where the neck starts."

He pointed in the opposite direction, toward the houses we'd passed when we first drove in. "Best spots are down thataway, though. Most expensive, anyways. Only you and one other house are this far south."

"I don't see any other house."

"Other side of the breakwater. Duh."

"Who lives there?" I had visions of an Elizabeth/Rachel hybrid. Maybe we could find a mall someplace. Ha! Probably wasn't one for fifty miles.

"Indian named Ben. He lives in a place that's shackier than yours. Up on stilts." Arthur guffawed. "Bright blue. Looks like a bird."

"Ben looks like a bird?"

"No, silly. The shack. Ben just looks like an Indian."

"I've never met a real Native American."

"I haven't really met him. But I've seen him a lot."

"Let's go over there, then," I said.

"My dad would skin me. Says the Indian is a little . . ." Arthur spun his finger in a circle by his head.

Oh, great. Stuck on an island all summer, with a crazy neighbor as a bonus.

"Do you fish?" I asked Arthur. This was something I figured I could do close to the water, without having to go in it.

"Yeah, but I didn't bring my stuff. Wanna swim?"

"Too cold," I said.

"Yeah," he said.

I shrugged. "Want to work on the dragon?" Arthur shrugged too, but he set to work. When we went in to get Popsicles the first time, my mom glanced up from her book and looked at Arthur.

"Is your dad Joey Ploof?" she asked. Arthur nodded.

"I went to school with him," she said. "You look just like he did."

"See, I said you weren't summer people," Arthur said to me. "I could tell right away you were one of us."

Either that made my mom laugh, or the expression on my face did.

Arthur and Beth stayed the rest of the afternoon.

At one point I asked him if he needed to let his mom know where he was for so long. He shook his head.

"Nah. She works until ten during the summer."

"Who takes care of you while she's working?"

He looked at me. "I do. And I take care of Beth, too, until her mom gets home."

Things were done a little differently here, I guessed.

When the sun got low, Arthur stood and looked up the beach. What had been a multicolored moving mass of people a couple of hours ago was empty except for the occasional body.

"We need to go home now. Maybe we'll stop back tomorrow."

Beth gave Free a hug, and she and Arthur headed up the island. I was surprised how sorry I was to see them go. Back home I would have been mortified to even be seen with the two of them, but I wasn't back home, was I?

Chapter 6

"I need some books," I said to Mom the next day.

"Good idea," she said. "I'll call the library and see what we need to do to get cards for us." When she got off the phone, she said, "You're all set. I went to school with the librarian, and she's letting us have resident cards. Tell Patsy hi for me."

"Where's the library?"

"Just walk across the causeway and it's on your right. It's not very big, but it has enough to keep even you in books this summer."

I stared at her. "Walk all the way to the mainland?"

She nodded. "You can't miss the library. Really."

"*Walk?*"

"Lise, how else are you going to get there?"

"Do you have any idea how *far* that is?"

"Yes, actually I do. I grew up here, remember? We must be less than a mile from the causeway, and the causeway itself can't be more than half a mile."

"You told me it was within walking distance!"

"It is. I used to walk it all the time. Sometimes two, three times a day."

"That was a long time ago!"

"What's that got to do with how far it is?" I didn't know, but she was still missing the whole point.

"Walk? With a load of books?"

"Of course."

"This is supposed to be a vacation," I said. "Not a forced march!"

Mom smiled. She *smiled*. When she saw how serious I was, she wiped it off her face.

"Lise, I think it might be good for you, honey."

"It's hot out!" I was whining now. Even I knew it.

"Then think how lovely the cold ocean will feel when you get back," she said, and I could tell from her voice that the discussion was over.

Hours are long when you're someplace you don't want to be. Long hours make for even longer days, but after a while my long days began to run together the way time always does. My skin turned sort of brown, nowhere near as dark and gorgeous as Free's, but at least I stopped burning. Free's hair was completely white now, and even mine had some sun streaks in it. The shells we collected filled our windowsills and outlined the porch and the steps. The grit of sand crept into our house, took up permanent residence in our hair, even got into our toothpaste.

"Extra crunchy," Mom called it. "Just like peanut butter. No big deal."

My life was falling apart. I had to walk miles just to get books to read, miles past nice houses with happy families, miles through groups of people playing volleyball who never asked if I wanted to play, miles along a ribbon of road where cars with out-of-state plates zipped by me and the kids inside ate ice cream in cushy air-conditioning. Tourists. Bleah. On top of all that, my teeth squeaked on grits of sand after I brushed them, and my mother saw no problem with any of this.

The rest of my summer yawned before me like a large and very empty bowl. Every day I woke up not knowing where I was, until I heard the relentless noise of the sea. It may not seem like an island would be that different, but it is. You're cut off, cut out, left out. I felt excluded, expelled.

You can't lie on your back on the beach and feel

the earth spinning, the way you can on a soft and grassy hill. Too much wave action, maybe, or too little contact with the rest of the continent, because instead of feeling rooted and connected, all you feel is surrounded and adrift. It was the longest, most boring summer I could imagine, and we'd only been there a couple of weeks.

Mom had gone funny on us. Before, on vacations, she'd been the most energetic of us all, always finding fun things to do and playing games with us. Now she spent a lot of time staring out to sea, and she seemed to think we should just amuse ourselves. I almost liked it better when she'd slept all the time. Free had gone a little different too. He didn't seem to mind the way we lived, and I didn't know what he was thinking all the time anymore.

I missed Elizabeth and Rachel. I missed Penny. I missed kids from school that I didn't even like. I missed my purple and red room with the tiny white Christmas lights. There was no cable TV here, no mall, no computer games, no Internet. Nothing else but the ever-present, inescapable ocean, for which I was supposed to be grateful.

"I hate this place!" I yelled one day in the middle

of making a mermaid. We'd gotten bored with drag-
ons and castles.

Free stopped and stared at me. I wasn't expecting
a response, of course. That's one of the great things
about complaining to Free.

"Mom's always staring off into space. She never
plays with us. I'm sick of happy tourists, I'm sick of
this horrible house. I'm sick of sand in everything.
I want to talk to my friends! I want to see a movie!
I want to go to camp! My life is ruined!"

I was shrieking by the time I was done, and Free
just stood there watching me. And then he did something he'd never done before. He ran away from me.
Not toward our house, not toward Mom, just away
from me.

Mom didn't fall, like Gray thought she might.
Although she moved painfully, and painfully slowly,
she did grow stronger. She had been pale since the
accident, but compared to the beach people, in their
various shades of red and brown, and even to me, she
was ghostly. White and unsteady, she shoved her
walker through the sand, up and down increasingly
longer sections of beach, her hair blowing in the

wind, her lips moving even when she was alone. People either looked much too long at the crazy lady with a walker and a big sun hat, or made sure not to look at her at all.

As if that weren't bad enough, Mom tied a big black trash bag to the front of her walker to collect beach garbage in. At first she made us go with her to pick up the trash, and I was relieved when she could finally bend down and do it herself. By then she had added a second garbage bag, and she pushed the walker with matching bags dangling from each side. I had always been proud of my beautiful, strong mother, but now she was gone. She wasn't even a normal frumpy mom now, like the mothers of most kids I knew. I was embarrassed by this hobbling woman who schlepped beach debris. I had to face the fact that I was now the daughter of a crippled loony.

The days didn't vary on Fiddle Beach. Free and I, and often Arthur and Beth, made sand sculptures or threw the tennis ball to Babe in the surf, or made crazy creations out of some of the garbage Mom collected—fanciful towers sporting beer cans, foam beer can holders, bright plastic buckets, shovels, a full-size broom, a plastic sandal, sunglasses.

"Trash into treasure," Mom said. "Brilliant."

Every night Mom had us push her wheelchair down to the beach, and she would sit and watch the sea until long after sunset, an old wool blanket around her shoulders. Although she didn't seem to mind us being around, she didn't talk much, and often she didn't hear what we said to her. Sometimes she nodded at something that only existed in her head, and sometimes she stared out to sea so intently that Free and I would look too, hoping to see whatever it was she saw, but we never did. So we never stayed very long and went back to the shack by ourselves. Sometimes Mom didn't start her torturous way back until Free was sound asleep, and the only reason I was still awake was because someone had to go fetch her wheelchair so the tide wouldn't suck it away.

At least there were Arthur and Beth, although I wouldn't have claimed either of them back home. Beth and Free usually went about silently building something in the sand while Arthur and I commiserated, and all of us ate vast quantities of Popsicles. My mom grumbled that the local teenager she'd found to deliver groceries from the mainland had to make twice as many trips because of all the

Popsicles, but you could tell she really didn't mind.

"The summer people think your mother's mad, you know," Arthur said. "That's what my mom hears." Arthur's mother worked at one of the local restaurants.

That made me glad the other beach people clustered together well away from our little piece of sand. There could be miles of empty beach, and still they clumped nearly on top of each other, their Frisbees colliding, their sand games overlapping, and the music from their boom boxes competing, as if they were afraid of a little open space. I hoped I was spared being associated with the ramshackle cabin with the bizarre junk art in front of it, and with my mother, who was looking more and more like a nutcase even to me. Still.

"My mom is crazy like a fox," I said. "Those people ought to get a life."

Mom didn't have to go to physical therapy as often as she had back home, but when she did go, we had to go with her all the way there and back in a taxi because there was no one she felt good about leaving us with. I hated those appointments. You could tell that Mom hurt afterward, and she looked tired and discouraged.

After her second appointment, Mom was "granny-ing," as she called it, her walker down the hospital hall, Free and me behind her, when a man with a clipboard and a stethoscope passed us in the hall. I felt rather than saw him watching us.

"Lise?" he said.

I stopped and turned around, wondering how he knew my name, but the tall man with the brown wavy hair wasn't even looking at me.

My mother steadied herself and turned slowly.

"Hello, Michael," she said. I didn't know what to make of the tone in her voice.

"What are you doing here?" the Michael guy asked.

"I had an appointment." Like, duh, I wanted to add.

"No, I mean here, in town. How long have you been here? Where are you staying?"

"Same old Michael. Never giving me a chance to explain."

"Same old Lise. Never explaining anything."

They looked at each other a moment. I thought they were both a little angry, until this Michael guy shook his head and smiled. Then my mom smiled too.

"What happened?" He gestured at her walker.

"Car accident."

"I'm sorry."

"It's not your fault."

"Well, at least something isn't." There was a silence after that. My mom looked away.

"I thought the sea air would do me good," Mom said. "We're here for the summer."

"That's great," Michael said, then he seemed to register Free and me for the first time.

"This is Freeman, after my dad," Mom said, "and my daughter, Lise."

"After you," Michael said.

"You look like your mom," he said to me. I didn't really, except for her perfect teeth and her long, thick hair—minus the gray, of course.

"But you, Freeman," Michael said, "you must take after your dad." At least he didn't squat down at Free's eye level.

Free just stared at him with his gray-green eyes, one eyebrow cocked a little.

Michael turned to Mom. "And their father . . . ?"

"He didn't come with us," Mom said. Technically this was true, but that wasn't what she usually said.

Another silence. I got the idea the Michael guy was looking for something in my mom's face.

"I didn't know you had moved back here, Michael."

"No," he said. "I'm sure you didn't."

Mom pulled herself away from the wall she had been leaning on and started to get ready to walk again. "Nice seeing you, Michael. Our ride is waiting."

He started to say something else, but stopped, then nodded.

"Good to see you, too, Annalise."

My mother didn't say anything the rest of the way home.

Inside the house I couldn't stand it any longer. "Mom, who was that man?"

"Someone from another life," was all she said.

Chapter 7

A couple of days later, Free and I were playing chess inside when I heard the screen door rattle. It was so loose that it just kind of shook in its frame when someone tried to knock. Michael stood there, peering in.

"Hi, guys. Is your mom around?" Babe had ripped a hole in the screen a few weeks before, and now stuck his head out in greeting.

"Whoa, back, beast!" Michael didn't seem the least bit distressed about the slobbery greeting or Babe's size. "What a beautiful big doggie!" he crooned, scratching Babe's ears. Babe's wagging tail beat my hip. It feels like you're being hit with a small pipe when he does that.

Mom had told me to tell everyone who called or came to the door that she was unavailable, whether she was available or not, because, she said, there was nobody on earth here she wanted to see or talk to. But today I was especially annoyed with her for moving us into this rotten house, instead of someplace near a swimming pool and within actual walking distance of a library, so I decided to tell Michael the truth.

"She's down at the beach."

"What's she doing?"

"Walking."

"By herself?"

"She says walking in the sand will make her leg strong."

Michael shook his head. "Maybe, but I don't think she's going to run any more marathons. It's a shame."

"Marathons?"

"She's never told you? That girl could run forever and hardly break a sweat."

Free and I looked at each other. Girl?

"Where's your dad?" Michael asked.

"Right this minute, I don't exactly know."

"I mean, does he live with you?"

"Why don't you ask my mom?" Sometimes it's fun making adults work for what they want.

"Because, knowing your mother, she wouldn't tell me." Michael smiled. "At least, not if I asked her directly."

"Then isn't it a little subversive of you to ask me?"

"You're not old enough to know what 'subversive' means, are you?"

"I'm old enough to use a dictionary, aren't I?"

"Well, aren't you the sesquipedalian one?"

"Can you spell that?" I asked him.

He stared at me a second, then threw back his head and laughed. It was a wonderful noise, and the sound of so much amusement caught me by surprise. I saw Free smile, and I realized I was smiling too.

"You are your mother all over again, aren't you?"

That pleased me.

"She says I'm a little wild," I confessed.

"Ha!" Another laugh came from deep down inside him. "Your mother grew up wilder than a rogue wave and about as strong. It will do the pot good to have a kettle as black as she."

I was silent, trying to figure all this out. Michael tried again.

"Do you ever see your dad?"

I had no intention of telling him one way or another, but from the corner of my eye I saw Free shake his head at Michael. I shot Free a glance, but he pretended innocence with those wide long-lashed eyes.

Michael nodded and fell silent too. It occurred to me

that two could play this fishing for information game.

"Did you know him?" I asked, trying to sound like this was normal conversation.

Michael shook his head. "Your momma moved away from here before she got married. I sure would like to know the guy who made her settle down."

"What makes you think she's settled down?"

Michael laughed again.

"I can see I'm going to have to be on my toes around you."

"That would be a good idea."

Michael waved and went off up the beach in search of my mother. I was surprised to see them coming back together after a while, my mother shuffling her walker in front of her, every step an effort. Michael was talking and gesturing a lot with his hands. My mom nodded occasionally. She was smiling.

When they got to the porch steps, Mom stood there, breathing hard. I knew she was trying to get the energy to make it up those three small steps. She would have to abandon the walker to do it, then hang tightly on the wobbly railing and pull herself up step by step. Michael stood there a minute, waiting for her to move, oblivious of the effort involved.

"You go ahead," she said. "I need a minute."

"Oh, here." Michael bent down and scooped her up, bridelike, one arm under her knees, one around her waist, then he hopped up the steps with her in his arms, one, two, three, just like that. He sat Mom in the rocker on the porch, then he retrieved her walker.

"Well, that was certainly easier." Mom laughed.

"You shouldn't be out there by yourself, Annalise."

"Why not?"

"What if you fall?"

"She'll just have to get up again, then, won't she?" I said. Michael and Mom both looked at me.

"Lise, could you bring the lemonade pitcher and some glasses, please?"

When I came back out, I heard her saying, "They won't even get in the water. I can't believe it. Nobody doesn't not like the ocean."

Michael squinted at her. "Too many negatives there, I think."

"You know what I mean. A summer on the coast and they won't even swim." It was the closest my mother had ever come to criticizing us.

"Not everyone has antifreeze in their veins, Annalise."

"We all played in the ocean for hours at a time, Michael, even skinny you."

"I wasn't skinny."

"Yes you were, and you still are."

"At least you're still looking at me."

My mother opened her mouth, then shut it.

"You win that round," she said.

"That's a first," Michael said.

A few days later Michael showed up again, this time with two funny body-shaped things.

"Wet suits," he said. "They won't keep you dry, but they'll keep you warm for a while."

"Michael," Mom started.

"Look, do you want them to enjoy the water or not?"

"Put them on," Michael said to us. We looked at Mom, who shrugged.

"Whatever."

We went into the house to change out of our shorts and T-shirts. The wet suits were tight but stretchy, and a little hard to pull on. Once inside, it felt like being wrapped in elastic. When we came outside in the wet suits, Michael was wearing only his trunks and holding two boogie boards. Mom was right. He was thin, but in a strong sort of way. And very tan.

"Follow me," he said.

"Tie Babe up first," Mom said. "Otherwise he'll try to rescue you and I'll have to dial nine one one."

Michael snapped the chain on the deck to Babe's collar, and then he ran straight into the water, the boogie board trailing from a leash on his wrist. No testing the water for this guy. Free and I followed him to the edge, me holding the second boogie board. We watched as Michael dove under a wave, and when we saw him next, he was farther out than we'd ever been, and Babe was doing his best to pull the deck off the house.

Michael stood about waist deep in the ocean, his body toward us, but looking back over his shoulder. Just as a wave appeared ready to crash over him, he launched himself. Michael rode over the lip of white foam, hanging on to the front of the boogie board, whooping as he flew. He landed a short distance from us, then stood and shook the wet hair out of his eyes, just like a dog.

"Who's next?" he said.

Free took a step and Michael reached out his hand. Together they walked into the sea. I watched as Free braced himself against the first wave, but he kept walking, even after he was soaked. I guess the wet suit worked. Once they got out to where Michael had been, Michael helped Free climb on top of the boogie board, and then held it in place until he saw a wave he liked. Michael gave Free a mighty boost and let go, and Free sailed even faster and farther than Michael had. The look on his face as he flew toward me said it all. I heard my mother laughing and clapping behind me.

"How is it, Free?" I asked. But I already knew. He stood up, turned around, and ran back to Michael with the boogie board on his wrist.

"Go on, Lise," Mom said. "You'll love it."

I sighed and began to wade into the water. Even though I felt a chill on my bare skin, with the wet suit on, the cold wasn't so cutting. I kept going, walking slowly. Unlike Michael and Free, I had on water shoes, and even then I felt bare and vulnerable, but at least with the wet suit there was a layer between me and the unknown. I let Michael balance my board and launch me just the way he had done with Free.

The first couple of seconds were awesome: pure flight. Then something happened. I thought maybe a shark bit me or the ocean floor blew up, but I guess I lost my balance and the board tipped. The next thing I knew I was spinning and twisting and sucking salt water up my nose. My shoulder hit the bottom hard and my feet went over my head, and I was left lying in two inches of water, stunned, gasping, and spitting.

"Get up! Quick!" Mom yelled, but I couldn't move fast enough. Another wave came and raked me over a few rocks. More water up my nose. My face felt dirty and tasted like I had popcorn grease smeared all over it. My eyes stung from the salt worse than they ever had from chlorine. Michael got to me before the next wave did and stood me up on my feet.

"Oooh, bad wipeout," he said. "It happens."

It would happen to me only once. I handed him the boogie board and walked over to sit with my mom.

"The next time will be great," Mom said. I shook my head. I felt something funny in my ear and I shoveled out some sand and a few tiny broken shell pieces with my little finger.

"Gross," I said.

As the salt water dried on me, I felt tight and

pinched and began to itch inside the tight neoprene suit. I watched Free and Michael playing in the water, jumping and splashing and flying, and I was a little ashamed. I saw my mother's glance linger on me a second before she smiled, and I realized something new and different: She was disappointed in me.

"I think I'll go for a walk," I said.

"Be back for dinner," was all she said, her eyes on Michael and Free.

I had no interest in watching the jolly families cavorting at the north end of the beach, so I took off south past our house. I kept going until I got to the breakwater, which seemed to be just huge chunks of rock and concrete piled up willy-nilly. I made my way up it, a little intimidated by the huge slabs and the deep pockets between them, holes big enough to hide a man. Standing on top of the breakwater, I saw for myself why the island was named Fiddle Beach. I was just above where the body of the fiddle connected with the neck. The way the breakwater extended from the mainland across the neck, I could pretend the line of rocks was a fiddle bow.

North, at the fat end of the fiddle's body, I could see cars on the causeway. To the south I could see to the end of the fiddle's neck, which appeared to just melt into the water. Large boulders like the ones the breakwater was made of dotted the fiddle neck. The only other thing on the neck was an old blue shack that sat about a quarter of the way between the breakwater and where the neck tapered into the sea. It wasn't built on the ground, but up on four stilts. Arthur was right. It did look like a bird.

I worked my way down the south side of the breakwater, which was even harder than going up, and began walking down the skinny strip of land. It was completely quiet except for the waves and a few gulls. I passed the shack, which seemed to hover about five feet above me. The door was closed and it was dark inside.

I walked and walked, surprised at how long the beach neck was. As the tide came in, I noticed the bar of land narrowed from both sides, not just the ocean side, so the tide seemed to rise twice as fast. I checked out a few tidal pools, found some baby starfish and one small lobster, then moved on down to the very tip of the neck, the very edge of my personal nowhere. I sat down on the sand and watched the waves. Farther north, the same wave motion was tossing my gleeful brother and that man Michael. The waves were pretty enough, and I was getting used to the sound, but I just wanted to watch the ocean, I didn't want to be in it. I'd never really been afraid of anything in my life, but this was different. Those waves were strong. They could kill you. And if they didn't, the things they carried could. Michael and my mother had grown up here, they should know that better than I. What was wrong with staying warm and dry? What was wrong with wanting to live where I finally had a chance for real friends? This wasn't the worst vacation in the world; it simply wasn't a vacation at all.

I saw something about the size and shape of a dime riding a wave in front of me. I thought it *was* a dime at first, but then realized that a coin wouldn't float. The tide started to pull the object back out; then, as if it had changed its mind, the disk came floating in again, settling exactly a foot in front of me. I cupped my hand over it, so it wouldn't drift off, and picked it up. I turned the odd thing over, then held it up to the sun. It was chalky white, with a flat bottom and a delicate star design pin-pricked into its curved top. I smiled at it in spite of myself and my mood.

"Looks like you got yourself a sand dollar," a voice

behind me said. Startled, I turned to see a man wearing a large-brimmed sun hat, a flannel shirt and jeans, and water shoes like mine.

"A sand dollar? Is it made of sand?"

"Nope. Made of calcium carbonate. That's quite a find for this beach. You find sand dollars all up and down the East Coast but hardly ever here, and if you do, they're very small like that. Some odd churning in the sea, along with a strange wind, deposits them here. I'd feel pretty special if I were you." He smiled, showing a small gap between his two front teeth.

Put that way, I did feel special.

"The tourist traps paint 'em gold to sell them to the summer folk, but I don't think there's any improving upon a shell."

I nodded and turned back to watch for more sand dollars.

"Of course, they're not really shells, you know. They're a whole different animal, closer to the sea urchin. The hard part is called a test."

"I've been here a few weeks, and this is the first one I've found," I said.

He sat down beside me and started to play in the sand, drawing lines with his finger the way a kid would.

"Are you here for the whole summer?"

"Yes. No. Not really," I said, wanting to explain that I wasn't a summer person, even though I was. "I mean, my mom was in a car accident and she thought it would help her recuperate to spend some time here."

"So you're like that sand dollar there. Something changed, and you ended up someplace you normally wouldn't."

I looked at him and nodded, thinking this was a fairly intelligent thing for an adult to say. His eyes were like an old dog's, crinkly and saggy, and a little watery.

I looked back at my sand dollar.

"I've noticed that the biggest, toughest shells are the ones that crack and shatter, but the light, little ones float above it all and land safe and sound. Odd, isn't it?"

I nodded again, pondering this, not finding anything to say in response.

"I'm Ben," he said. "I live in that house over there."

"You're the Indian?" I said, before I thought. "Native American, I mean."

He laughed. "Well, I'm one of them. I'm a Passamaquoddy."

"A what?"

"Passamaquoddy. It's a tribe."

"I haven't ever heard of that one."

"How about Abenaki?"

I shook my head.

"Abenaki means 'People of the Dawn.' There are a number of tribes in the People of the Dawn. Passamaquoddy is just one of them."

"I'm Lise. We live in the shack on the other side of the breakwater." I didn't mind admitting it to him, given what his house looked like.

"That shack has been there since well before most of those grand homes," Ben said. "It may not look like much, but it's stood the test of time. It's the real thing."

Real what? I wondered.

"You been swimming?" Ben nodded at my wet suit.

"First and last time boogie-boarding," I said. "Give me a swimming pool anytime."

"What's the difference?"

"The ocean scares me."

"Why?"

"I'm afraid I will die out there." It was out before I could stop it. Why I could say this to a man I didn't know and not to my mother, I can't explain.

Instead of laughing or looking alarmed, Ben

nodded. For the first time I noticed a black braid trailing halfway down his back.

"You don't think that's silly?"

"Of course not. What is silly are those fools who don't understand that the sea can take a life. I've seen a lot of them, too close to the rocks on their surfboards, or too far out in a tide stronger than they are, too drunk on their boats to swim if they had to. Can you swim?"

"Of course," I said.

"Well, that's something," he said. "I never learned."

"And you live right on the water?" This seemed really stupid, even for an adult.

"I'm an edge person," Ben said, as if that explained everything. And to me, it did.

"I don't get it. Everybody here is wild about the ocean."

"The sea is part of our history, it is deep within all of our memories. Some people believe we learned to stand on two feet not so we could throw spears but so we could walk deeper and deeper into the food-rich sea. It makes sense to me—think how easy it is to support your own weight in the water."

"I like that better than the idea that we learned to stand up so we could hunt."

"I do too," Ben said. "The sea is generous to us."

"It's too big."

"It's big, it is. And it can be cruel, too. Those of us who live on the coast know that firsthand."

"So why do you stay?"

Ben shrugged. "Every place can be both cruel and generous. The ocean is what it is."

I looked at the sun. "I should be going now," I said.

"If you'd like, ask your parents if you can come see my beach treasures sometime," Ben said, gesturing toward his bird house. "I have some old artifacts, too, if you're interested in that sort of thing."

"I'd like that," I said. He tipped his floppy hat at me, and I took off toward the breakwater.

"Take care of that sand dollar," he shouted after me. "They're fragile."

I tried, but the sand dollar was white powder in my palm by the time I'd made it to the top of the breakwater. It was one of those days. No, the whole summer had been like that.

Chapter 8

The beach north of the breakwater was almost empty, but when I got to the house, my mom and Michael were on the front porch. Didn't that man have anywhere else to go? Free was on his belly by Babe, reading one of my science fiction books. Aliens and hostile foreign lands seemed to fit my mood these days.

"Those waves are mighty strong, aren't they, Lise?" Michael said as I came up the stairs.

I wanted to tell this guy not to be patronizing, but something told me Mom might take a dim view of that. Instead I just nodded.

"She'll get the hang of it," Mom said. I knew it was supposed to be encouraging, but she was missing the point. I had no desire to get the hang of it.

"I'm not going in that water ever again."

"Why ever not?" my mother said.

"Because I'm an edge person," I said.

Mom started to protest, but Michael held up his hand.

"She's entitled," he said.

"But the water is where all the fun is," Mom said.

Michael shook his head at her.

"The edge is where things meet. Interesting things happen on the edge. Lise just likes her terra firma."

Mom looked at him funny. So did I. We weren't used to anyone intervening in our family squabbles. I started through the door.

"Lise, honey," my mom said. "Bring me a beer when you come back out, please?"

"You shouldn't be drinking alcohol with those painkillers, Annalise," Michael said.

I stopped. I wasn't used to anyone telling my mother what she should and shouldn't do.

My mother eyed him back. "If they're called painkillers, then why don't they kill the pain?"

Michael held her gaze for a moment, then looked away.

"Never mind, Lise," Mom said. "I'll get it myself." She hoisted herself up and guided her walker into the kitchen.

Michael looked at me and shrugged. "She's pushing too hard. No wonder it hurts."

"She says she's getting stronger. She sure moves better than when we got here."

Mom came back with two glasses of lemonade. She handed one to Michael. "I'm not happy about it, but you're right."

"What do I know? I'm just a doctor," he said.

"And don't you forget it," Mom said. "People make their own choices, Michael."

Michael looked away and took a sip of lemonade. I thought it was a good time to change the subject.

"I met the man who lives on the other side of the breakwater," I said.

My mom looked at Michael.

"Ben's still alive?" she asked.

"Oh, very," Michael said.

"But he was ancient when we were kids," Mom said.

"Everybody is ancient when you're a kid. Still, he is getting up there. The diabetes is taking its toll too."

"Arthur said he's crazy," I volunteered. *He said everyone thinks my mom is crazy too*, I thought. But I didn't say it.

"Sounds like something Joey Ploof would say,"

Mom said. "In fact, I think I remember him saying that exact thing when we were younger. Joey was dumb as dirt then, and I bet he's dumb as dirt now."

"Ben's far from crazy," Michael said. "He knows more about the tides and the beach than the rest of the town put together."

"Well, he ought to move inland," Mom said. "That house can't keep him very dry in the summer or warm enough in the winter. He's getting too old to be living that way."

"People make their own choices, Annalise." Michael made a face at her and Mom stuck her tongue out at him. Even Free and I didn't do that anymore.

"Why didn't they build the breakwater south of Ben's house?" Mom asked.

"It wouldn't have protected the rest of the island as well. They tried to get him to move, but he wouldn't. You know what he's like." Mom nodded.

"He said I could come see his shells and stuff, if it's okay with you," I said to Mom.

"Sure. Ben likes honey in his tea. Take the new jar in the pantry."

"Annalise, he's diabetic," Michael said.

"That never stopped him before."

Michael rolled his eyes. "I know, I know—choices."

"And I found a sand dollar," I said.

I might as well have said I'd found buried treasure.

"Show me!"

"I crushed it getting back over the breakwater."

"Oh, well. There'll be others," she said. "Where did you find it?"

"Other side of the breakwater."

"I always loved finding sand dollars, but they've never been very common here. When I was little, I decided they were good luck, especially when the tide plunks them right at your toes, as if it knows you're waiting for them."

"Ben said they only show up if something stirs up the currents, or an unusual wind blows."

"He would know, he's watched this beach long enough," Michael said.

"He also said something about the big, heavy shells getting broken, but the little ones floating safely in."

Mom looked at me thoughtfully for a moment. Then she nodded.

"Ben knows a lot about a lot of things. You guys have a good talk?"

"I guess."

"The best time for sand dollars is low tide," Mom said. "A lot of people will walk right by them. It feels as if only you can see them sometimes. Like they find you, instead of the other way around."

I knew just what she meant, but I don't think she was really talking to me. Or to any of us.

I found two more sand dollars the next morning. At low tide, just like my mom said, lying in the sun like ancient treasure coins. I held them carefully in my cupped palm all the way back home, taking no chances this time.

Mom wasn't there, just a note that she and Free had gone walking, so I wrapped the sand dollars in tissue and tucked them and the jar of honey in my backpack. I climbed up the breakwater, pleased that I made it to the top a lot faster than yesterday. I could see Ben sitting at the edge of the water, fishing, or at least holding a fishing pole. I don't know if he heard me over the surf, or just felt me there, but just as I got down the other side, he turned toward me. I waved. He waved back, then reeled his line in and started walking in my direction.

When I reached him, I handed him the honey.

"My mother said you liked honey in your tea, even though you shouldn't have it," I explained, wishing I hadn't said that last part.

"How would your mother know I like honey?" Ben asked, then smiled. "No. The right question is '*How would she know I shouldn't have it?*'"

"She said she knew you from when she was growing up on the mainland. Her name is Annalise LaMer. She didn't change her name when she got married," I remembered to add.

"Annalise?" Then, "Oh, you mean Lise!" He brought his face close to mine, and I could see how hazy his eyes were.

"And you're her daughter. I should have known. Same name and you look just like her. I guess that makes you *petite* Lise." Ben handed me his fishing pole and, opening the jar, stuck a finger in for a taste. "Well, *petite* Lise, we'd better have some tea, then."

We walked back to his bird house. He was a little slow going up the steps, thinking about every one. It reminded me of my mother.

He gestured for me to sit at the single chair at a tiny table with a blue metal oil lamp on it. Not just *on* it, *nailed* on it. Ben saw my glance.

"Gets breezy in here. And sometimes the house wobbles at high tide."

Wobbles? Geez.

Ben turned to a camp stove that was set up on a board jutting from the wall. He pumped the stove up, lit the burner, then dropped a few marbles in a pan of water and put it on to heat. He pulled up a rocking chair and sat across the table from me.

I laid out the two sand dollars side by side and pushed them over to him, smiling.

"Well, you have been busy! And very lucky."

I told him about my mother's tips.

"Trust Lise to remember."

"How well did you know my mother?"

Ben shrugged. "She was one of the many beach rats who have hung out on Fiddle Beach over the years, doing things that would worry their parents. Usually she was with a tall skinny kid. A fisherman's son who became a doctor."

"Michael," I said.

Ben nodded. "That's right. Lise was one of the few kids with any time for an old man, an Indian at that. She loved the sea, that one. I wasn't surprised to hear she'd left, but I didn't think it would take her this long to come back."

"What was my mother like when she lived here?"

Ben laughed. "Wild as hell and twice as angry, but don't tell her I said so."

"My mom? Angry?"

"She's changed, then?"

I thought about it. "No, she still gets angry, but usually not at my brother and me."

"That's good. Sometimes angry people end up hurting those they love most."

"Why did she leave here if she liked it so much?"

Ben shrugged. "The ones who stay don't have many choices. They become fishermen, or waitresses, or clean hotel rooms for minimum wage. Hard lives. Your mother, I seem to remember, wanted more."

"But why didn't she ever bring us back to visit? Maybe this summer wouldn't be so bad if we were used to it."

"It depends on why she left. Maybe she was afraid that if she came back, she might never leave again."

And I knew when Ben said it that he was right. That's why this didn't feel like a vacation, because Mom acted like it was home. I'd probably spend the rest of my life in that horrible shack, serving lobster and clam chowder to the summer people. Marry Arthur and have a bunch of kids dumber than dirt.

"You said she had an accident?" Ben said. I guess I'd been silent a long time, contemplating my future as a waitress.

I told Ben about Mom getting broadsided, her wheelchair days, her walker. And I didn't stop there.

"I hate everything about being here. I had a perfectly good life where I was. I was just starting to fit in, and now here I am in this nothing place completely cut off on all sides by water. I don't want things to change!" I was near tears when I finally stopped and stared at the table, trying to keep from bawling.

"They already have," Ben said, and the sheer truth of this fact quieted me.

The marbles in the pan rattled, and Ben got up to make the tea. Unlike the tidy, self-contained tea bags my mother used, Ben's tea was loose and leafy, and he shook it into our cups from jam jars. The liquid he gave me was spicy and gold colored. I noticed his was a deep black. Ben spun a rope of honey into his cup, then another. He pushed the honey jar toward me, and I did the same. We didn't say anything for a while, but it wasn't a bad silence.

"I'm sorry you're unhappy here," Ben said "We all go through things we don't enjoy, but usually you can find something to make it more bearable."

"Nothing can make this more bearable. If I make one more sand castle, I'm going to puke."

"That *is* serious." Ben grinned, gap-toothed. I got an image of me puking on my next sand castle. I grinned too.

Ben reached out and selected a small sea urchin from the bookshelf beside him and placed it by one of my tiny sand dollars.

"Why is it these delicate little things arrive on Fiddle Beach whole, and bigger, thicker shells end up broken or crushed?"

I shrugged. Ben waited.

"Maybe the weight of it, the size."

"The bigger they are, the harder they fall, right? So maybe going with the flow is sometimes better than trying to fight it."

I had him there. "But if you go with the flow, a strange current can pick you up and take you far from home. Like the sand dollars, like me."

Ben nodded. "That's absolutely right. So there are physical things we can count on, and there are things we can't control. A lot in life just happens, doesn't it?"

"I'll say."

"Your mother couldn't control what happened to her, but she is doing what she can to make it better. And she needs your help."

"I could help her a lot more if we were back home."

"That's the point. She is back home. I know it's not your home, and so does she, but I bet she knows what she's doing. She may not even know she knows, but she does. Maybe you need to try changing what you can instead of what you can't."

"There isn't anything I can change!"

"There is always something that you can change. Everybody has times when it feels like the pieces of their life have been tossed in the air. When the pieces land, they need to be fit back together. Sometimes the pieces fit pretty well; other times, they don't seem to fit at all. You may just need to work to fit those pieces together, but sometimes you have to change the pieces."

I think I had just been told to stop whining, but I wasn't sure. Boy, this wasn't what I'd come to see Ben for.

"Of course, that wasn't what you came here for," Ben said. "Come, look at my beach treasures. Do you have a sea glass collection?" he asked, reaching for a jar on the windowsill.

"Not really. I've picked up a few pieces, but that's all."

"Then you have a sea glass collection." Ben dumped the jar out on the table. "Light green is the most common here on Fiddle Beach. Blue is the rarest."

We sorted through the various bits of glass, the soft tinkle soothing to hear, discussing the merits of the different colors, pondering how long each piece had been tumbled in the surf, wondering if they had once been beer bottles or pirate's plates.

"Pick a few pieces you really like for your collection," Ben said, as we started to put them back into the jar. When I hesitated, he said, "The whole point of having things is to share them, right?"

When I was ready to leave, I took one of the sand dollars from the table and pushed the other toward him. Ben smiled.

"Thank you," he said. Then, as I started down the stairs, "And thank your mother for the honey. Tell her that she has always been a very strong person."

Chapter 9

That next weekend Michael showed up with a skim-board and a kite.

"Lots of things to do on the edge, Lise," he said. Although he said they were for Free and me to share, it was obvious what he was trying to do. What was less obvious was why.

Free wanted the skimboard first, so Michael and I went north a ways to launch the kite away from the electric line. It was a good kite, taking to the wind more easily than any I had ever flown before. I felt the strong pull of the kite on its string as the colored parafoil rose higher and higher. I wished I was up there with it. I wished I could fly on the wind. Fly home. But if my mom and Free were here now, wasn't that where home was supposed to be?

"Just out of curiosity," Michael said, "what in particular don't you like about the ocean?"

I had to hand it to him. He knew how to distract his prey before pouncing on it.

"For one thing, it moves all the time."

"That it does. Some people think it's soothing. People pay good money just to feel themselves rocked in a boat."

"Cradles rock. The ocean slaps."

"Depends on where you are. My dad always used to tell me that under the surface, the ocean was calm as could be. What else bothers you?"

"There's things in there," I said.

"What are the kinds of things that bother you?"

"Squishy things. Sharp things. Maybe even sharks. I've read about sharks. My mother says there's never been a shark attack up here," I said, before he could say it, "but they could still be out there."

"You have a better chance of being hit by lightning than being attacked by a shark up here."

"It doesn't matter if there aren't any sharks if it feels like there are," I said.

"Fair enough," Michael said. He gestured toward the water. "It's a big unknown, Lise. What lies beneath gives everyone the shivers at some point or another. It's like the dark in a way. But the only thing you really have to be concerned with here is the cold water. It can kill you, for sure. You and your brother stay close in and wear those wet suits."

"They itch," I said.

"Deal with it," Michael said. He sounded just like my mom. I looked at him, annoyed. He winked at me.

Michael showed up at our shack a lot more often than I thought was necessary. His schedule at the hospital was erratic, and sometimes his beeper went off shortly after he got to our house and he left right away, but sometimes he stayed for hours. And he always came back.

"Why does Michael keep coming over?" I asked Mom one evening when she seemed more like her usual self than she had in a long time.

"Why not?" she said. "We've known each other a long time. He's certainly been good to you kids—he knows this summer hasn't been easy."

"Hasn't been easy?" I couldn't believe that's how this disaster of a summer appeared to her. "It's been miserable!"

"Lise, really," Mom said. "No one can be miserable

spending a summer at the beach. My accident has been hard on all of us, but it's a beautiful spot, Michael's done nothing but give you attention, you've made friends—"

"Friends? What friends? All the seagulls? They're the only ones who don't notice I live in a dump."

"You know who I mean. Arthur and his cousin. You spend half your time with them."

"Only because there's no one, absolutely no one, else. I wouldn't be caught dead with either of them back home."

"Then you shouldn't be caught alive with them here, Lise," she said. It was not an approving tone. "Besides, what about Ben? He's been your buddy."

"Ben's an old man. And Arthur makes fun of me for talking to Ben."

"Let me get this straight, Lise. Someone you wouldn't be caught dead with makes fun of you for being with someone you enjoy. Maybe you need to think for yourself a little more. And you seem to have developed a pretty serious case of self-pity."

Well.

"Anyway, Michael is helping me a lot. He's helping *us* a lot. I appreciate that, and you should too. I haven't gotten better as quickly as I thought I would."

"Free and I can do anything you need done," I said. "We never needed anyone before your accident, and we don't now."

Mom started to say something, then stopped, and her face changed from looking like she was ready to argue to something else, something almost sad.

"Come here, sweetie," she said, and when I did, she hugged me hard and close. "You're my best girl," she said. "You always will be."

I wanted to be angry with her, but I didn't know why, or really what about, so I just let her hug me. It felt good.

"Can't I go back home, just for camp?" I asked.

She looked at me, that old look again.

"I need you here, Lise," she said. "There's so much I can't do for myself. If you weren't here, I don't know how I could cope."

What can you say to that?

"It's not fair!" I said.

Mom nodded. "You're right. It's not. But it is what it is."

And what can you say to that?

One afternoon Free and I came home from getting ice cream at the Beach Bum to find Mom and Michael in the water. She was hanging on to a boogie board, and Michael was steadying her on the surf. A wave came up and Michael let go of the boogie board. I couldn't imagine what he was thinking, turning a crippled woman loose on a raging monster wave. Mom hung on tightly and the wave deposited her in a pile on the beach with a plop. Free and I ran to her from one direction, and Michael bodysurfed to her from the other. We arrived at the same time, gasping and breathless, where Mom lay on her back. I thought she was crying at first, but when I got close enough, I saw that she was chuckling to herself. She was wearing a swimsuit for the first time since the accident, and the ugly, puckery scars on her leg from the surgery were out in the open for everyone to see. Gross.

"That was a good one," she said to us all.

"What are you doing?" I asked.

"Isn't it obvious? I'm boogie-boarding."

"But you can't even walk right yet."

"I don't have to," she said. "That's the beauty of it."

Michael took over. "Your mom thought the cold

water would numb her leg and give her some relief from the pain. So she sat in the water, and then she wanted to float, and one thing led to another, and . . . " He shrugged.

Then he picked her up, bridelike, and still laughing, she put an arm around his neck and there was that pose all over again.

"Just like old times," he said.

Chapter 10

A couple of days later, Michael was working on replacing the door frame and installing a new screen door. It was his day off, but it wasn't a weekend. He had the oddest schedule with the most bizarre hours. Free was in the house with Beth, teaching her to play his keyboard. I envied them their silent, sweet friendship. They were alike in some ways: trusting, innocent, a little out of step with the world. Or maybe just in step with a different world. Arthur and I were working on a sand sculpture. We had decided to make a loggerhead turtle, because it had the advantage of not needing to be too tall. Arthur and I got along okay most of the time, but sometimes things got a little prickly.

"Ben says that maybe people learned to walk on two feet from wading in the ocean looking for food."

"Why would you listen to what a crazy old Indian has to say?"

"He's not crazy."

"My dad says so."

"Maybe your dad's the crazy one."

"No, remember, your mom is the crazy one."

"My mom is the one who got out of this dump of a town."

"And she's the one who came back, too."

"At least she's not going to stay."

"My mom said your mom was nothing but trouble all through high school." I wondered what kind of trouble, but figured I shouldn't let on I didn't know.

"Who cares what your mom thinks? She's spending her life spooning mashed potatoes. At least my mom has a life!"

"Well, at least my mom has a husband!"

"If my mom wanted a husband, she'd have one!" At least, I thought she would.

Arthur didn't respond to that. We were close to knocking each other down, but I don't think either of us really wanted to. I know I didn't. I wasn't sure why we were fighting, or exactly what we were fighting about. I guess he wasn't either, because when I stepped back, he did too. But he started in again.

"I wouldn't listen to a thing Ben says. He's nobody,

and he's a nobody who's been nowhere."

"Everybody is somebody. And Ben's happy doing what he's doing. What's wrong with that?"

Arthur sulked. "I still say he's crazy."

"Crazy is as crazy does," I said. I had no idea what it meant. Neither did he, I could tell.

Arthur stood and kicked at the turtle, taking out the head I'd been working on.

"Hey!"

"I'm sick of this," he said. "Let's go get ice cream at the Beach Bum."

"It's too far. I just walked to the library yesterday."

"I'll ride you on my bike," he said.

"I don't have a helmet."

Arthur looked at me. "Stupid. I don't either."

"My mom won't let me on a bike without a helmet."

"So," Arthur said, "don't tell her."

I looked at him. I hadn't ever lied to my mom, but I was sick of sand sculptures too.

"I'll go tell her we're leaving," I said.

I don't know whose dumb idea it was. I know it didn't seem dumb at the time. I don't even know if Arthur wanted to take the stuff primarily because he thought it was cool, or because he actually wanted the stupid colored zinc sunscreen and the chocolate bars and didn't have the money to pay for them. Whatever. I had the money in my wallet, *in my wallet,* and still I let him convince me it would be nifty to slide the tiny items into our baggy shorts pockets. And so easy. And it was. I felt delightfully evil afterward, knowing I was walking around the Beach Bum with stuff in my pocket I wasn't going to pay for. I, who had been brought up to be painfully honest, had finally gotten over it. I wasn't the least bit bored anymore. I felt proud.

Until we passed the cash register and started to walk out the door. Mr. Towler, who owned the Beach Bum, said, "You two, stop right there."

Like idiots, we did as we were told, but hey, that's how both of us had been brought up.

"You gonna pay for that stuff?" he asked. Neither of us said a thing. I don't know about Arthur, but I was simply too scared to find any words that made sense. *Yes, but we forgot? No, we weren't?* And then what?

"Back in my office, you two," Towler snarled. He was a grumpy man to begin with, never smiling even when you were handing him money, and now, especially when we weren't. He marched us through a narrow little door into a cramped office that looked like a bale of paper had exploded in it. There was no place to sit, so we stood, shoulder to shoulder against a back wall.

"Empty those pockets." We did.

"Wait here," Towler said, and he shut the door.

Arthur looked like he was going to cry.

"My dad will whip me," he said. "*Whip* me. I mean it."

I got an image of Officer Ploof, as big and tall as he was, with a whip. Arthur was even skinnier than I was; there was absolutely nothing to cushion the cut of any blow. My mother had never struck me in my life, and all I knew about being hit had come from hitting first. Far too soon Mr. Towler opened the door again.

"It was my idea. It was all my idea," I said. "I'm sorry, but don't punish Arthur. Punish me instead."

I could see Towler would rather take it out on the crazy lady's kid than one of their own, the town cop's own at that.

Arthur held his breath.

"Run along home, Arthur," Mr. Towler said. "I don't want to see you in here the rest of the summer."

Arthur ran out. He didn't look back.

"And you," Mr. Towler said. I looked at him with what I hoped was an expressionless face. Adults don't like it when you look them in the eye. He wanted me to be frightened, and I was, but I wasn't going to give him any satisfaction by showing it.

"You'll just have to sit tight for a while and contemplate your sins."

He left me, shutting the door again. I looked out the window of the smelly office and was surprised to see that the sun was shining very brightly. Inside that office, however, it was a very dark day. I wondered if I would go to jail. I wondered if Free would be allowed to visit me there or if, like the recovery room, they had a minimum age for visitors. I had wanted my mother to be very sorry that she ever brought me here, hadn't I? Be careful what you wish for.

After what seemed like an extraordinarily long time, I heard Mr. Towler's voice outside the door. I couldn't hear my mother's voice, but I could tell from the little indignant squeaks he was making that he was describing my wretched crime in great and exacting detail. When the door opened, though, it wasn't my mother who stood there, it was Michael.

"Come on, Lise," was all he said.

I stared with hard eyes at Mr. Towler so he wouldn't know how close I was to crying. Michael put his arm around my shoulders. He bought Popsicles on the way out and we must have looked like just a couple of tourists, and for this I was very grateful. Free was in the car when we got there.

"Where's my mom?"

"She had to go to physical therapy, remember?" Michael said. "I told her I'd come get you." We drove home in a silence broken only by soft slurps on Popsicles.

Michael continued to work on the door when we got home. Free handed Michael stuff as he asked for it, but after a while my brother got bored and took the skimboard down to the water. I don't know why I hung around, but I didn't want to be by myself, and I didn't want to be alone with Free, who kept giving me funny looks. Michael worked in silence for a few minutes after Free wandered off.

"Did you do it because you didn't have money, Lise?" he asked, his back to me so he was talking to the door frame.

"No," I said. "I had money."

"Just wondering," he said, talking to his saw now.

"Never steal something because you don't have money. Money is an easy thing to fix." Michael paused, then glanced up at me. "It's the other stuff that isn't so easy."

And it was the other stuff I'd been trying to fix, I knew. He did too. I nodded and turned away, but he had seen the tears leaking down my cheeks.

"Sweetie," he said, turning me around and pulling me to him. I buried my face in his chest and he rubbed my back. I hate to cry. I never cry. I can't remember the last time I cried. But Michael didn't seem to mind. He just rocked me side to side a little, and when I was done he found a clean bandanna for me to blow my nose on. I stood there for a long time, leaning into his chest, listening to my breath and his. Finally I stepped back. He looked at me.

"You gonna live?" he asked.

I nodded.

"We need to go get your mom pretty soon. Run get your brother for me, okay?" he said.

I wanted someone to yell at me and tell me what a disgrace I was so I could yell back and tell them it was all their fault. Instead, when we picked up Mom, she decided we should go out for pizza, and after that she declared she felt well enough to go to a movie. By this time I had convinced myself that she was unaware of my crime, or had misunderstood the nature of it. Maybe Mr. Towler had spoken only to Michael, and Michael had chosen to delay telling Mom the details. Maybe he could even be convinced not to tell her the whole gory story. I was even surer of this when Michael winked at me while we waited in line to buy popcorn. When I just looked at him, confused, he reached over and ruffled my hair.

"Hey," he said, "life isn't so bad."

"Maybe yours isn't," I said. "But mine sucks."

Michael laughed. "Remember my dad used to say that under the waves, the ocean was calm as could be?"

I nodded. But what did this have to do with the price of peaches?

"It was his way of saying that sometimes you need to go a little deeper for the peace and quiet."

I didn't get it.

"You know what else he used to tell me?"

"What?"

"That sometimes it's okay just to float."

"Float how?" I wasn't getting in the ocean again.

"Stop fighting, let the drift take you where it goes.

Save your energy and let things happen. You might be surprised."

That night, stuffed from pizza and popcorn, tired from staying up later than usual, I lay in bed wondering how I'd gotten myself into this whole predicament, when shoplifting had never interested me before and definitely never would again.

I finally heard Michael's car leave, and still my mother didn't call for me to come down to talk to her. Surely the time for ranting and raving had passed; I had dodged the bullet on this one. Maybe there really was a god. I heard Mom rattling around the kitchen, talking to Babe, rustling a newspaper.

I had almost drifted off when I heard Mom start to pull herself up the loft ladder. She had only climbed it once—to make sure the loft was safe for us to sleep in—and I'd been surprised that it was actually easier for her than regular stairs because she could use her arms. When her head poked into view, I saw she had her pajamas on, and I could tell by the smell that she had washed her face and brushed her teeth for bed. Somehow, though, she wasn't surprised that I was still awake. It was as if she'd expected me to be. She swung herself off the ladder onto the loft floor, then scooted in close so she could brush the hair from my forehead. She did that silently for a few moments, and it reminded me of the times I was sick with fever and she would stay with me for hours at night just to comfort me.

"Everybody makes mistakes, Annalise. In this family everybody gets one free one. This one was yours." Then she kissed me and left.

She never calls me Annalise unless it's serious.

Chapter 11

Arthur and Beth didn't show up the next day. I guess I wasn't surprised, but still, it would have been nice if Arthur had checked up on me. For all he knew, I'd been whipped myself or spent the night in a jail with rats. Or both. I guess that's why he didn't show up.

Michael and Free were boogie-boarding and my mom was off on a garbage walk, so I took the skimboard down to the shore, but got bored after a few slides. I scrambled up the breakwater and down the other side and walked quickly to Ben's house. He answered the door as if he were expecting me, and he beckoned by pointing to the single chair.

"What's on your mind?" he said.

"What makes you think anything's on my mind?" I asked, suspicious. For a second I wondered if Mr. Towler had called everyone and broadcast my offense, maybe even put it in the local paper.

"You look like a person with something on your

mind," was all Ben said. I had to accept that.

"I did something really wrong yesterday," I said.

Ben just looked at me.

"I mean really, really wrong."

"And?"

"And my mom didn't even punish me."

"Are you going to do it again?"

"No!"

"Sometimes we punish ourselves plenty without needing someone else to do it for us."

"What do you think I should do?"

"I think you should have some tea," he said.

As Ben busied himself with the tea, I looked at the contents of his shelves. There were kinds of shells I'd never seen on Fiddle Island, a few old-looking books, some pictures. I stopped at a photo in a cheap wood frame. Three men in uniforms with palm trees behind them.

"A much younger me," Ben said as he handed me my tea, the gap in his teeth the same as the man's in the middle of the photograph. "Hard to believe I was so thin, huh? No wrinkles then. Lots of strength. I have the hat still, but the uniform is long gone."

"I thought you'd lived here all your life."

"Why would you think that?"

"I don't know," I said, but I did. Arthur telling me the crazy Indian had never been anywhere or done anything. I bet it was Arthur's father who had never been anywhere or done anything. "Where was this taken?"

"Hawaii," Ben said, and did a little hula motion with his fingers.

"Hawaii! Why did you come back here?" I couldn't imagine anyone returning to Fiddle Island once they had escaped. I tried to picture Ben wearing hula garb, drinking from coconuts, surrounded by pineapples, and I could see it just fine.

"Why not? I've never needed anything that wasn't here," Ben said. "Hawaii's coast was very nice, but the sea there just didn't sound right to me."

"It didn't sound right? It all sounds the same, doesn't it?"

Ben shook his head. "This," he said, pointing out his window to the Atlantic, "sounds like *natick*."

"Natick?"

"Home," he said.

"Where else have you been?"

"After Hawaii, I went wherever I was told to go."

"Did you like those places?"

"The places were fine," he said, "but I never did get used to being a soldier."

We honeyed our tea and sipped in silence for a few moments.

"What can you tell me about sharks?" I asked.

Ben's face crinkled and he reached for his neck. From it he pulled a thin leather strap, and from that strap dangled a triangular tooth at least an inch wide.

"You didn't get that here, I hope," I said, with that awful gut feeling.

"No, not here. It's a Hawaiian shark, or one that was passing through that way. There were all sorts of shark tales in those waters. Sharks that could stop the propeller of a boat with their mouths, sharks that jumped right into boats, sharks that swallowed men whole. There can be sharks in almost any waters, Lise. They are the top of the food chain, except for man."

"I don't want to hear this, do I?"

He went on as if I hadn't said anything. "They often swim on the fringes of beaches, almost as if they are guarding. Guarding the swimmers or guarding the ocean, who knows? Of course there are sharks here. Not many, or not many we see very often.

They're supposed to be there. But just because they are there doesn't mean they will hurt you."

I just looked at him.

"A certain amount of trust and courage is required to live in this world, Lise. Or rather, to live well."

"So what am I supposed to do? Trust that they won't eat me and then be brave when they do?"

"Just accept them. Everyone has to get out of bed each day and accept things we don't particularly like. Everybody has their own sharks."

"What are your sharks, Ben?"

He smiled.

"I, too, used to be afraid of the ocean."

"You?" I was amazed, but then the more important thing he was saying dawned on me. "Used to? When did you stop being afraid? How?" I hoped his answer would provide the magic I needed to be able to run and splash and surf in the sea like Michael and Free did, the way my mother used to, the way she wished me to now.

"I completely lost my fear of the ocean when I acknowledged that it is where I will die."

"What?" I don't know what I expected, but this wasn't it.

"The ocean will take my life." Arthur was right. Ben was crazy.

"How do you know?"

"I know the way we know all important things. I just know."

"But why then do you live here? Right here? You could go away, far away, where you can't possibly die in the ocean."

Ben shook his head. "Only my shell will return to the sea; part of me will always be part of this world."

"Why? When you are given that kind of knowledge, it's foolish not to use it." I was angry.

"But I do use it. Every day." He paused to sip his tea. "It is a gift to know your death."

"I don't think so!"

"In knowing your death, it is easier to know your life."

"I don't want you to die."

I saw a flash of white teeth. "You need, Lise, to make your desires a little more realistic. Don't worry—as long as I wear my shark tooth, the ocean can do me no harm."

"Then never take it off."

"Now, why would anyone want to live forever? When I'm too old to fish, too blind to see my beach and pick up the garbage on it, I've done all I can do in this world. We're all part of the plan."

"What if I don't like the plan?"

Ben smiled. "Sometimes you can bend it a little, but you have to know when to fight for what is important to you, and when to accept the plan."

"Will I die in the ocean?" It was worth a shot asking him, I figured.

Ben smiled, and shook his head a little. "I do not see the future, *petite* Lise. But I think it's possible for us each to know our destiny."

"How?"

"Do you believe you will die in the ocean?"

"Sometimes."

"When the time is right, you need to ask the ocean. And it will tell you."

I looked right into Ben's black eyes, trying to see inside his life, his world, his fears. Ben held my gaze with a deep, unblinking stare. Only my mother and Free had ever before allowed me such a glimpse into them. Now Ben.

I smiled and blinked. Ben smiled too.

"Drink your tea, *petite* Lise. Perhaps it will give you a clue."

I looked at my mug. It was almost empty. "My tea? How can it tell me anything?"

Ben shrugged. "Perhaps not."

He reached for my mug and peered into it. He swirled it a few times and sat it down on the table again in front of me. I watched the leafy sediment in the dregs swim and spiral and finally settle into a simple ring around the outside. Nothing unusual about that, since the edge of the mug was lower at the outer rim. But as I watched, an image appeared. Like a developing Polaroid picture, five elliptical shapes came into view, and together with the ring they made the perfect pattern of a perfect sand dollar.

Chapter 12

I had almost stopped thinking constantly about my previous life, when I got a postcard from Elizabeth. She was at rock-climbing camp. My rock-climbing camp. It made me sick to think of all the fun she was having there. Without me. Rachel had gone in my place to the camp, and Elizabeth was going to take my place with Rachel at art camp. When I got back in the fall, they would be so close that there wouldn't be any room for me. Rachel and Elizabeth would have great stories of their exploits, and I would have nothing but sand in my pants. I hadn't seen the new movies; I hadn't been to a mall in *forever*. I hadn't even had any fast food since we got here. I was losing the little I had gained, I was losing everything. What really got me, though, was the last line of Elizabeth's postcard: "Poor you—I bet they don't even have fireworks up there."

I looked at the calendar. July 3. The Fourth of July

was a big deal in our house. To me it was one of the best parts of summer, and in some ways summer didn't even begin in my mind until July 4. How could summer only be beginning when I'd been on this tiresome island for at least a century? On all the other Fourths I could remember, we had picked a mountain to climb, or gone on a long hike or bike ride. We would find salamanders and trillium and all sorts of cool things and eat chocolate bars for energy, coming back close to dark, hot and exhausted and very giddy with our adventures. We always had something great for dinner, like store-bought fried chicken, and then we'd go watch fireworks, the three of us snuggled in a fuzzy blanket. I knew of no other way to spend the Fourth of July, and apparently—since she didn't mention any celebration—neither did my mother.

But Michael did.

He picked us up on the morning of the Fourth with his motorboat in tow and a car filled with food— one cooler entirely full of soda, the other full of lunch and treats. My mother gave him a look as Free and I settled into the back of his car with a can of soda in one hand and a candy bar in the other, but Michael grinned at her. To my surprise, she just grinned back. I was even more surprised when Michael unsnapped Babe from the deck and loaded him in the back of his station wagon.

"We can't leave him here," Michael said. "He's family. Besides, he'll love it!"

"What if he jumps in the water?" I asked.

"Then he'll swim."

"What if he tips the boat over?" I asked.

"Then we'll swim," Mom said. "Joke!" she said, when she saw the look on my face.

"There's no way he can tip the boat over, Lise," Michael said.

"Promise?"

"Pinkie-promise." And he did.

We drove to the boat access, and Michael backed his boat trailer to the edge of the water. Free and I helped him get the boat in the water, then Michael helped Mom into the boat. Then he issued life jackets, and while Mom slathered sunscreen on us, he revved the motor and we took off up the coast.

When we pulled away from the shore, it struck me again that anything could be carried by these waves— toward you, under you, over you, all around you. There was no escape. What if the boat swamped far from shore? What if we had engine trouble and we drifted for days and days? I wondered if we would drift north toward the pole or south toward the tropics. It didn't matter, really, no doubt we'd die either way. Or what if a storm came up and we sank? The sky *was* cloudless, but you never know. Mom and Free were so excited that I would have felt stupid saying anything, so I didn't. And Michael did seem to know what he was doing, but . . . you never know.

Babe walked from one end of the boat to the other a few times, then positioned himself standing with his front legs up on a seat cushion, his nose into the wind. As we picked up speed, his ears flapped and drool blew off of him. He looked supremely happy. After a time passed and disaster didn't strike, even I had to admit that being out in the hot sun on top of the water with the sea breeze cooling us felt good. No, it felt great.

In the translucent crest of one of the waves, I saw dozens of small silver fish arcing like eyeless eyebrows. Michael pointed to the distant breach of a whale, and a few porpoises followed us for a while, dancing in our wake as if inviting us to play. Not a single shark appeared. None that I saw, anyway.

At one point I saw a person swimming and I waved. The swimmer didn't wave back, and then I realized that he or she was too far from shore to be safe. The form moved slowly with the slosh of the sea, and as we came closer, I noticed there were no rhythmic strokes of the serious swimmer, no steady kicks. The shape was dark and still, moving only on the motion of the waves. Floating. I felt a chill panic.

"It's a body!" I yelled. Mom and Michael stopped talking and looked where I was pointing. Michael put Mom's hand on the wheel of the boat and came over to Free and me. The body disappeared, then suddenly surfaced a little farther north.

"A harbor seal!" Michael said. "Good eyes."

Sleek and shiny, dark and fat, the seal bobbed up and down in the waves, looking pleased with its joke. Free tugged Michael's shoulder and pointed in another direction.

"Jellyfish," Michael said, looking at the clear, pulsing blobs. "You know what you call a bunch of jellyfish?"

We shook our heads.

"A smack. Like a pod of whales or a school of fish. A smack of jellyfish."

"A crash of rhinoceroses," Mom said.

"A romp of otters," Michael countered.

"A riot of children," Mom said.

"I haven't heard that one," he said.

"I made it up. Just now."

"A grit of sand," I said, getting into it.

"A clatter of shells," Mom said.

"A bunch of loonies," Michael said. Free laughed out loud.

"What's so funny, kid?" Michael said. "No laughing on this boat. It's against the rules. I'm the captain and I should know." Michael stood and grabbed a giggling Free, then turned him like a pinwheel until he was upside down. He looked really funny with all that white hair hanging down. Free was laughing, so hard it was the silent kind of laughter, and the look Mom gave Michael and Free made me think I could probably get away with another soda and candy bar.

I was right.

A little later I looked around and realized I could see nothing but water. Sun on the water, wind on the water, us on the water. Nothing but water.

"Where are we going?" I asked.

"I don't know," Michael said, scanning the horizon. "I think we might be a little lost."

The expression on my face must have been something, because he said, "Joke. Just a joke!" And within a few minutes he pointed to a small island in the distance.

"How did you know that was there?" I asked. He hadn't used any charts or maps that I could see.

"Magic," he said. "I'm good, huh? Even Houdini couldn't produce islands on demand."

The island drew closer and Michael threw an anchor out. The three of us splashed out in a foot or so of water, and then Michael helped my mom out. We had the entire island to ourselves. Cool.

Michael had brought an amazing lunch. Crab salad, corn bread, soft and chewy chocolate chip cookies, wild blueberries. Wild blueberries are tiny and tart, not those sweet balloons you got in the grocery store where I came from. More soda, more candy bars. After lunch Mom stretched out on a large tilted slab of rock to soak up the sun. Babe plopped down beside her.

"Take them to see the old foundation," Mom said to Michael, and I realized this wasn't the first time they had been here.

"Let's explore, guys," Michael said. We followed him, but I didn't see a path. He pointed out an osprey nest in the dead white limbs of the tallest tree on the island. Then he grabbed some lichen he called old man's beard off a spruce tree and held it to his chin, then to Free's. There was a shrill, weird cackle, and Michael stopped talking to scan the horizon. He pointed the loons out to us and didn't start speaking again until the loon's crazy sounds were almost too faint to hear.

We walked until we came to a short wall, no more than a few inches high, nothing more than a line of rubble.

"This island belongs to the state now, but when your mom and I were in high school, an old French-Canadian woman named Angelique Marie lived here. All by herself. When she was young, she married a Passamaquoddy. It didn't make her family happy at all, so they moved out to this island, all alone. When he died at sea, everyone thought Angelique would move back to her people, but she didn't. She had a small hut and she paid my dad to bring her water and whatever else she needed. If it was his busy season, sometimes your mom and I would bring her stuff out instead. She always gave us homemade root beer. It was always cold—I never did figure out how she managed that.

"Whenever we came, she was always wearing the same dress and the same hat. And lipstick. Do you believe that? She always had on lipstick. We thought it was strange, but it took me a long time to realize just how strange it really was."

Michael stopped talking and kicked the wall with his toe.

"I don't know what she did to keep warm in the winter. It had to be wicked cold out here."

"What happened to her?"

"There was a storm," he said. And then he stopped.

"And?" I said. I hate it when people make you pry the next part out of them.

Michael shrugged. "That's it. There was a storm." He kicked the wall again. "This is all that was left."

What he was saying sank in, and I realized there was no next part. I shivered.

"Maybe she spent the storm on the mainland. Didn't your dad come back to see if she needed help?"

"Angelique didn't go to the mainland. There wasn't

any warning that the storm was going to be so rough."

"At least he could have checked!"

"Well, he didn't," Michael said.

"Why not?"

Michael didn't answer me right away. I knew he'd heard me because he was looking at me. He kept looking at me, then he finally spoke.

"Because he died in the storm that night too."

My eyes went wide, and I remembered Ben telling me that Michael was the son of a fisherman.

"Was he fishing?"

Michael nodded. "Went out that morning and just never came back."

I knew how that felt.

"I'm sorry," I said.

"Me too," Michael said. Free slipped his hand into Michael's and Michael draped a hand around Free's shoulders. Michael kicked the wall one last time and we headed back to my mom and Babe in silence.

I was more than a little relieved when Michael docked at a marina. Terra firma. I still preferred it, especially after Michael's story about his father and Angelique Marie. Michael roped the boat up, and we walked on the beach. The day had gotten even hotter and the beach was belly to belly with holiday people. Kids were yelling and running all over the place, leather ladies glistened in bikinis, and some of the men did too. Startlingly white skin seemed to turn pink before our eyes, like shrimp boiling. Bellies wobbled, thighs rippled, bottoms hung out, tops spilled over.

"I bet you haven't seen so much white meat since Thanksgiving," Mom said, smiling at the look on my face.

"The smell of suntan lotion always makes me hungry," Michael said. "How about you guys?"

There was no way anyone could be hungry after that lunch, but Michael treated us to ice cream anyway. I asked for a banana split as a test, and sure enough, he didn't bat an eye. Free's eyes went wide.

"Free wants one too," I said.

"You're spoiling them, Michael," Mom said.

"That's the idea," Michael said. She raised an eyebrow at him.

Free and I looked at each other. "Works for me," I said.

It was a short boat ride back to the access ramp and Michael's car, and from there we drove back to Fiddle Beach, where we made a sand castle to beat all other sand castles, complete with sparklers in the turrets. Michael built a bonfire on the beach ("Don't tell anyone," he said, with a straight face) and we cooked hot dogs and s'mores. After dark we lit the sparklers on the castle and set off a few firecrackers Michael had sneaked in from Canada.

When it got too cool by the water, we went into the house and Mom turned on the radio to hear the weather forecast. What came on instead was one of the songs we had always cleaned house to, back when we had a real house, back when my mom had the energy to clean. I started singing to it, and Free started tapping his foot to the music, and Mom nodded her head in rhythm and clapped. Michael took her by the hands.

"Dance!" he said.

"I can't!"

"Say what?" Michael said, his hand behind his ear as if he couldn't hear her. He pulled her to him and slipped his feet under hers, and he spun her around like she was one of those dancing dolls that you strap on to your legs.

"What are you doing?" Mom shrieked, but we could tell she was loving it. Michael held her to him with one arm, and she didn't have to do a thing but hold on tight, which looked kind of tough because she was giggling so much. In turn, Michael put Free and me on the tops of his feet and whirled us around, stomping in rhythm to the music, and when he went back to Mom, I put Free on the tops of my feet and did the same with him. When the song got to the saxophone solo, Free broke away from me to play air saxophone. He got the moves just right. I mean, he was *good*. Michael had to put my mother down because he was laughing so hard. The song ended too soon, but we found some others that were just as good.

I forgot I was miserable, I forgot I hated my life. The music was loud in the little shack at the south end of the north beach, and the lights there burned brightly late into our Fourth.

Chapter 13

The next day my mom sent me over to Ben's with the leftover wild blueberries. When I got to his house, I climbed the steps and knocked on the wall, since the door was already open. I saw Ben rise from the rocking chair, where he had been staring out his window to the sea, and I noticed how he stopped partway up, then gave himself a little push to make it the rest of the way. He seemed slower today, stiff. His foggy eyes lit up and he reached for the blueberries with an eager hand.

"I was just thinking it was time for the early blueberries," Ben said, popping some into his mouth. "Your mother and I must be connected somehow. They say great minds think alike." He smacked his lips and reached for more. "Up until a few years ago, I walked to a patch on the mainland to pick these. It's a shopping center now. I haven't found another spot close enough for these old legs to make it to."

"Michael said he would take us picking soon. You can go with us then," I said.

Ben motioned me in. I bet those berries were gone in less than three minutes.

"I went out on a boat yesterday," I said, trying to lick the purple off my fingers with no success. "You wouldn't believe the things we saw." I told him about the whale, the porpoises, and the harbor seal. "It was pretty cool."

"Are you going to give the ocean another chance?"

"As long as it behaves, we get along just fine," I said. "But Michael told me about his father and Angelique Marie. It seems like people who trust the ocean die too young."

"It happens," Ben said. "Now, Angelique Marie, there's a name I haven't heard for quite a while. She was old when I was a kid."

That's what my mom had said about Ben.

"I bet Angelique thought she was too young to die."

"Maybe, maybe not. What kind of boat were you on?"

I shrugged. "A boat's a boat, isn't it? That reminds me. My mom said you used to have a boat, but I don't see one around."

"I sold it last year."

"Why?"

Ben smiled and looked out to sea. "If I had a boat, I'd be tempted to use it. It's better this way. I can't use something that isn't there."

"Why did you stop, if you didn't want to?"

"I can't see well enough anymore to be safe. I might cause an accident or hurt somebody. The time to quit is before you wish you had. That way you don't ruin the good memories with bad ones."

"Do you regret that you sold it?"

"Regrets are a waste of time."

"My mom says that too."

"See? What did I tell you—great minds."

"But how do you get off the island?"

Ben pointed to the breakwater. "On top of that."

"You climb the breakwater and walk?" I asked. He was too old and rickety to be messing around on the breakwater. "What if you fell?"

"Then I'd just have to get up again, wouldn't I?"

I stared at him. "You sound so much like my mother, it's scary."

Ben laughed. "Must be something in the air."

"Maybe you should get a canoe at least," I said.

"You know, a long time ago the people who lived here fished from dugout canoes. Can you imagine being in some of those waves in a canoe?"

"In the ocean?" I asked. "I don't think of Indians as fishing in the ocean—more like hunting in the forest or the plains, maybe catching a few fish in a river."

"The People of the Dawn had many lifestyles and a lot of different skills," Ben said. "The Pennacook, Maliseet, Micmac, Penobscot, and Passamaquoddy are just a few of the tribes. Some took seal with harpoons, some speared lobster with long staffs." He turned around and took a long toothed thing from the shelf behind him. "This is a bone point from a harpoon. Wouldn't you like to know what it's seen?"

I took the bone from him and turned it over. It was so warm it felt alive. I wondered who had had the patience to carve such minute points on it—I wanted to know what they had been afraid of, who they had loved, how they had died. I looked up to see Ben watching me.

"They speak, these things, don't they?" he said. I nodded.

"What do you make of this?" he asked, handing me a funny-shaped rock, fat and spherical on the top and bottom, worn thinner in the middle.

"Some sort of toy?" I hazarded. "Although you could probably kill somebody with it too."

He pulled another, similar one from the shelf, and this one had a middle notch wound with cord that was attached to a businesslike hook. "Fishing weights."

"Now this, it isn't as old as the other things," Ben said, removing a tall basket from where it was hanging on a wall, "but it is very special to me. My mother made it."

He motioned for me to stand up, and he slipped a strap over each of my shoulders.

"It's a pack basket," he said. "Lots of kindling I've carried in this."

In spite of the fact that it was made from wood, it was very comfortable, just like my backpack.

"My mother taught me how to make baskets, although I was never as creative as she was. In her day men didn't weave baskets, but she was concerned that not enough youngsters were learning the skills. A few are trying to keep the ways alive, but one day all that may be left of us are our words on maps."

"What words?"

"Well, 'Taconic' for one. It means 'wilderness,' not a highway in New York. And 'Winooski' means 'wild onions,' not just a river in Vermont. 'Nashua,' 'Saco,' 'Acadia,' 'Yankee'—all our words."

"'Squaw,'" I said.

"'Squaw,' Lise, is one of those words we won't take credit for. It's not a nice word."

"Oh," I said, embarrassed. "I didn't know."

Ben patted my hand. "At least now the state has changed all their squaw place names to something else. Most white people don't know it's a nasty word."

"I'm sorry," I said. I was.

"Just like they don't know that natives were not made citizens of this country until 1924."

I burst out laughing. He eyed me.

"That's ridiculous!" I said, and Ben grinned, showing me the gap between his teeth.

"Yes, it is, isn't it?"

He turned and opened a wooden chest by his cot. From it he pulled the most beautiful thing I had ever seen. He saw the look in my eyes and smiled.

"Touch it," he said. I reached out one hand to feel the soft hide decorated with beads and something else. I looked more closely.

"Porcupine quills," he said. "I caught the porkies myself."

The robe felt so soft and luxurious that I reached out my other hand and brought it to my face to inhale the rich, sweet smell.

"It's gorgeous!" I said.

"It is," Ben agreed. "My ceremonial robe. Not much call for it these days, but I put it on when I'm feeling especially grand. Or nostalgic." He rummaged around some more in the trunk and came up with two deer-hide tubes decorated in the same way as the robe.

"Leggings," he said as he handed them to me. "And moccasins. The last pair my mother would make. Although I didn't know that at the time."

"This is better than a museum," I exclaimed, reaching for the well-worn moccasins.

"They belong in a museum." Ben nodded, turning away. "But not yet."

"Not yet," he repeated, so softly I almost didn't hear him.

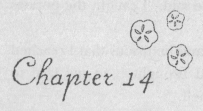

Chapter 14

Mom did something unheard of. She left us for a whole day. I don't mean left us alone. Of course not. She had this notion that she had improved so much from her beach walks that she could get rid of her walker and go to a single crutch, but both Michael and her local doctor disagreed with her. So, being my mom, she decided to find someone else to "discuss it" with. She was going to a big orthopedic clinic, and she'd worked out the appointment and the bus and taxi arrangements all before saying a word to any of us.

"I would have driven you up there, Annalise," Michael said. I knew miffed when I heard it.

"I know you would have, but I need you to watch Free and Lise," Mom said. "That's why I made the appointment on your day off." She gave him a little smile. It wasn't her usual confident smile; it looked more like mine when I was trying to get away with something.

Michael looked at her.

"I can't take them with me, Michael. The bus ride would seem like forever to a kid, and they would be miserable. You're the only one I trust enough to leave them with."

They were both silent for a moment.

"You always tell me that I never ask for help when I need it, Michael. I'm asking now." I'd seen Mom get her way with a lot of people before, but this soft-sell approach was something new.

When Michael didn't reply, Mom said, "Okay, okay. I'm sorry I asked. They'll just go with me."

"That's not the issue, and you know it."

"Then what's the issue?"

"It's too early to give up the walker. If you won't listen to me, can't you listen to your own doctor? You'll fall and re-injure yourself, and then where will you be?"

"Then you can say I told you so."

Michael threw his hands in the air at that.

"Annalise! The last thing I want to do is say I told you so, I want—"

"You want me to do what *you* want me to do. You always have. This is my body, Michael. My future."

"You don't listen to anyone who doesn't agree with you."

They each had their hands on their hips by now.

"Neither do you! I may take what I want, Michael, but I pay for it," Mom said. I was afraid this was a reference to my escapade at the Beach Bum, but apparently not. "I always have. You know that."

Michael's jaw was clenched, and I could see the muscles in it working. Mom and my dad had never argued that I could remember. At least not like this, with loud angry words and tense faces. I started to feel a little sick to my stomach. Michael closed his eyes, but my mother just continued to stare at him.

"You drive me nuts, you know that?" he finally said.

My mom relaxed, even though, to me, Michael still looked furious.

"Then you'll do it?" Mom said.

"Of course I'll do it. You knew from the start I'd do it, and so did I. That's why you drive me nuts," he said, shaking his head.

"It's not a bad kind of nuts, is it?" Mom said.

"It's the worst kind of nuts there is, Annalise."

But he smiled as he said it.

So that's how I ended up helping Michael replace the steps to the front porch. Mrs. Lafayette was more than happy to let him put in new, shallower steps and a sturdier railing that would make it easier for my mom to climb them. We'd done the measuring (twice) and the cutting (once) and were now finally making stairs.

After a while Michael stood up and stretched and looked to make sure Free was still where he said he would be boogie-boarding. Babe was tied up next to us and he didn't like it one bit—his eyes never left Free, and he whined occasionally.

"Why are you smiling?" I asked Michael.

"Do I have to have a reason?"

I nodded. "There's a reason for everything."

"You are one tough twelve-year-old," he said, smiling. I realized I had raised an eyebrow at him.

"Okay," he said. "I'm smiling because I'm glad you and your mom came to Fiddle Island. You and Free are both great kids."

"Doesn't it bother you that Free doesn't say anything?" I asked. Sooner or later, that always came up with people.

Michael picked up his hammer and turned back to the steps. "Did you ever hear the joke about the kid who didn't say anything until he was six?"

"I don't think so."

"One day he announced that his toast was burnt, and his mother said, 'Oh, you can speak! Why haven't you said anything in all these years?' And the kid replied, 'Because everything was fine up until the burnt toast.'"

It wasn't really a good joke, but I could see Free pulling something like that. I wondered if Free would think the joke was funny. I wondered what it would take to finally start Free talking, and what would happen if my mother was wrong for once and Free remained silent the rest of his life. It occurred to me then that my mom must have talked to Michael about Free. About Free and maybe some other things.

"You know why my dad left, don't you?" I asked.

Michael froze. His face was still, and his muscles weren't moving because all his energy was being used up by the spinning in his brain. Adults do that when you catch them off guard, and it's always a little funny.

Michael looked down at the sand. He didn't look at me.

"It doesn't matter now, does it?"

"That he left, no. What matters to me is if my mom told you why he left."

"I'm sure your mom will tell you someday if she wants you to know."

"Oh, I already know."

"You do, do you?" I know Michael thought I was pretending, thought I was trying to get him to spill the beans.

"He left because he didn't want another baby. He didn't want to spend the time, the money, the energy."

"Your mother told you that?" Michael looked appalled.

"Of course not! She would never say anything like that. It wouldn't be appropriate." Michael smiled at this. I knew he was hearing my mother's voice say those exact words, just like I was.

"I heard them," I explained. "He said, 'You can't have both of us, Annalise. Either the baby or me.'" There were other words too, but those were the ones that stuck in my mind the most. I remember too the days after those words, when the house was silent and still even though they were both there. I remember the car ride my dad took me for a while later. 'I will always love you and we'll see each other a lot.' And I never saw him again."

"You heard them? You were what—six? seven?"

"You won't tell Mom, will you? She thinks I don't know. She would die if she thought I knew."

"What reason did they give for your dad leaving?"

"The usual. 'Sometimes mommies and daddies don't love each other anymore but he will always be your dad,' blah blah blah." I knew enough kids whose parents were divorced to know it was the standard line.

Michael eyed me. "You're a scary kid sometimes, you know?"

"Thank you."

"Were you sad when your dad left?"

"Only for a little while. Then Free was born and things got busy."

"You ever miss having a dad?" Michael said. It was a serious question, but he was pretending it was small talk.

"No," I said. "Never." That shut him up. He didn't need to get any ideas.

After a minute I felt a little bad for him and relented.

"You like my mom, don't you?"

"Of course I like your mom. Duh." Michael was holding a couple of nails in his mouth, and it made a funny twist as he talked.

"I mean . . . a lot."

"You think she likes me . . . a lot?"

"Well, at least she . . ."—I sought the correct word—"tolerates you."

Michael spit the nails out of his mouth, threw back his head, and laughed. I loved that laugh, but I had no idea what was so funny.

"What do you mean, 'tolerate'?" he asked.

"Hell, any other guy, she'd be slamming the door in his face." We bent down to pick up the nails together.

"Your mom does that?" He looked at me. He didn't even tell me to watch my language.

"Has. More than once."

"Why?"

"She says . . ." I paused to get it right, because it never made much sense to me. "She says a woman needs a man like a bicycle needs a fish."

Michael didn't laugh like I expected him to. People laughed when Mom said it, but now that I thought about it, she only ever said it to women.

"I think the phrase is 'like a fish needs a bicycle,'"

he said. Then he stood up. "What else does she say?"

"That she has an unfortunate penchant for men who don't want to be fathers."

He ran his fingers through his sweaty hair, and I could see where it was starting to go gray above his ears. He was quiet for so long I got a little uncomfortable.

"You tell your mom something for me?"

"Maybe."

"You tell her that people change."

"Okay. But what's a penchant?"

"You're the kid with the dictionary. Go look it up." He was a little cranky all of a sudden.

"When's my mom coming back?"

"Not until mid-evening."

"What about dinner?"

Michael grinned. Whatever had ticked him off was past. "I make the meanest boiled lobster in the county."

"We haven't had lobster yet." I'd seen them in the Fish Market, where I went to buy lemons for all the lemonade we drank. They piled up like pigs in the corner of Plexiglas tanks, rubber bands around their claws. I was surprised when I found out they were still alive. When I asked my mom about buying some, she said, "Maybe in a restaurant sometime. I don't like to cook them."

Michael crooked his finger at me. "Come see."

He led me inside the kitchen and opened the refrigerator.

"Ta da!" There on the middle shelf, in the largest clear bowl I had ever seen, were four lobsters covered in water.

"Are they alive?"

Michael looked at me like I was nuts. "Of course they're alive."

"Aren't they . . . a little uncomfortable in there, then?"

"You're the girl who thinks the ocean is freezing," he said. "They live in it, remember?"

Free came running in from outside and skittered to a stop when he saw the lobsters. He giggled, came closer, and reached out to touch one.

"Watch their claws," Michael said. "They're banded shut, but those guys are fresh this morning and still pretty feisty. I've seen one of those dudes snap a plastic spoon in two."

Free and I stood back in respect.

"Want to see how to hypnotize a lobster?"

We nodded.

Michael selected one from the bowl and shook off the water. The lobster moved his? her? legs in agitation. Michael held it under its belly, then began rubbing the top part of its shell back and forth, back and forth. Free and I watched as the lobster's legs slowed until they finally stopped moving completely and hung loose and lazily from its bizarre body.

Free giggled again as Michael replaced the lobster in the bowl.

"Nothing better than fresh lobster and hot butter," he said. "Nothing in the world."

"How do you eat it?" I asked.

"With these," Michael said, producing nutcrackers and nut picks from a bag on the table. "I'll show you. Pretty soon you'll be doing it like a native. It's pretty funny watching the tourists make a mess of themselves. And the amount of lobster they waste is a disgrace."

"They look like they're all shell," I said.

"Just like the polar bear said about the humans in the igloo: crunchy on the outside, chewy on the inside."

Free wrinkled his nose.

"That's sick," I said.

"Here's another one: A cannibal walks into a bar. What does he say?"

I thought. I'd heard some jokes about men walking into bars, but I don't remember punch lines very well.

"I give up."

"Ouch!"

"What's the matter?" I looked at Michael. He didn't appear to be in pain.

"Nothing's the matter, silly. It's the punch line."

Free and I looked at each other, then Free started laughing. Hard.

Michael started laughing at Free.

"I don't get it," I said. That made them both laugh harder. I thought about it again. "I still don't get it."

I hate it when Free understands things that I don't.

Chapter 15

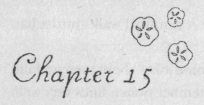

After we finished the steps, which probably took longer than it should have because both Free and I were "helping," Michael brought an enormous pot from his car. He filled it with water, then had me add salt to it and put it on the stove to heat. While we waited for the water to boil, he and Free worked on a salad, and I sliced and buttered bread. As the water started to steam, Michael melted butter. Free and I set the table. By now I was starved.

"*Mademoiselle et monsieur*," Michael said, bowing from the waist like a fancy waiter. With a flourish he took the lobster bowl from the refrigerator and picked up one of the lobsters. He swept the lobster in front of us, its claws moving rapidly. It wasn't hypnotized anymore.

"Say hello to dinner," Michael said, smacking his lips.

He turned back to the stove and lifted the lid on

the pot, which was now full of spitting and popping boiling water.

"Always remember to put them in headfirst, otherwise you'll get splashed. That hurts." Michael lowered the lobster in, quickly followed by the other three.

"Aren't they still alive?" I said, certain I'd missed something.

"Of course they're still alive!" Michael said, exasperated.

That's when the clicking started. From inside the pot. And that's when Free started screaming. No words, of course, but he didn't need any. Michael turned in alarm. It sounded like Free was in pain. I guess he was.

"What's the matter?" Michael said, rushing to Free. But Free put his fingers in his ears and ran into the corner of the other room. He crouched down facing the wall and began sobbing. Outside, Babe began barking and scratching at the new screen door, trying to get in, frantic to rescue somebody from something.

"Lise, what's the matter with him?" Michael yelled. In a panic. And he's the doctor.

"It's the lobsters," I yelled back, not believing this guy. How dense could you be? "Turn it off, get them out of there! You're boiling them to death!"

"Of course I'm boiling them to death!"

"He doesn't like it! I don't like it! Stop it!"

Michael looked at me with wide eyes, then he ran back to the stove and moved the pot off the burner. The clattering continued. Free kept crying. Babe kept barking. With some effort, Michael heaved the pot to the sink and poured the water out, then dumped the lobsters into the garbage. When the clicking ceased, Free's sobbing stopped, leaving only that funny kind of wet breathing. Michael went to him and put his arms around him.

"It's okay now, Free," he said. "I'm sorry it scared you. It's how you cook lobster. Honest."

"That's gross," I said.

"Try killing a cow sometime," Michael snapped. "You don't seem to have any problem eating hamburger."

"At least you don't boil a cow to death. How would you like to be cooked alive?" I said, my hands on my hips.

"You sound exactly like your mother!"

"Good!" I said. His eyes flashed and he stood up so quickly I thought he might hit me, but instead he walked out the screen door, letting it slam hard behind him. I saw that Babe had already ripped the new screen.

"Shit," I heard Michael say. That seemed a little extreme for a piece of ripped screen. I watched Michael sit down on his new steps and put his head in his hands.

"Shit," he said again. Babe flopped down at Michael's feet, placated but exhausted.

I got a tissue and went to Free, who was still huddled in the corner.

"Free, he didn't mean any harm. It was supposed to be a treat," I said. Free wiped his eyes on the back of his hand. I handed him the tissue and he blew his nose. Then he got up and went out the door and sat down by Michael on the steps. Michael didn't move, so Free put a little hand on Michael's back and patted him softly. After a moment Michael pulled Free to him with one arm and they sat there, rocking a little, arms around each other.

"Why didn't I just stick to crab cakes?" Michael said. Nobody answered him.

"We still have salad and bread," I said, a little tentatively, because there was something here I didn't quite get, something more than just dinner.

"No, that's okay," Michael said, sighing. "Pizza or burgers, guys?"

"Pizza," I said. His comment about hamburger bugged me. We drove to the pizza place in silence. Free and I were quiet the entire meal. Michael didn't even try to talk to us, and I began to respect him a little more. An adult who actually knew when to shut up.

It wasn't until dessert that he said anything. "Sorry, guys. I never thought about it like that before." Free, who was sitting by him, just reached for Michael's hand. He had forgiven Michael, but I knew he would have nightmares that night.

"Buds, Lise?" Michael said.

"I can't believe that's how you really cook lobster," I said, but Michael knew I was just trying to goad him, and he didn't give me the satisfaction of a response. Maybe he was brighter than I'd thought.

When Michael opened his wallet to pay for dinner, I saw a picture, just a glimpse, but enough to know it was my mother's senior high school portrait, the one where she looks like a movie star. Michael caught my look.

"Here's another," he said, flipping to the next one. It was a picture of him, standing on the beach. Longer hair, no gray yet, an even darker tan. In his arms, in that bridelike position, was a laughing woman in a bikini. My mother.

"Didn't know she was a beach bum, did you?"

I pursed my lips.

"My mother in a bikini. How disgusting."

Michael held it out in front of him for a better look. "Really? She looks pretty good to me."

He flipped to another. Michael in a suit, my mom in some slinky dress. She had a corsage on.

"So, was she, like, your girlfriend for a while?"

"Your mother was the love of my life," Michael said lightly, but I knew he was not kidding.

"Thank you, Doctor Mike," the waitress said, big smile, touching Michael's arm. "Come see us again real soon."

"You're welcome," he said, without looking at her. I could tell she was a little put out when she walked off.

"So what happened?"

Michael snapped his wallet shut and didn't answer me. We were out of the restaurant and walking toward his car before he said anything.

"Sometimes, at one point in your life, things can seem very important, and then later you wonder why you made such a big deal about it."

Free and I looked at each other. I didn't have a clue what he was talking about. Michael tried again.

"When you're young, it's easy to convince yourself that you're right, when really, you're just being selfish."

He looked at us. "This isn't making any sense, is it?"

We shook our heads.

"What it boiled down to is that both your mom and I were just too stubborn."

Free and I nodded. That was something we understood.

We went to pick my mother up at the bus station. She came toward us slowly, no walker in sight, only a single crutch. Her face was ecstatic.

"So, you got what you wanted," Michael said, as he helped her into the front seat.

"Don't I always, Michael dear?" Mom said.

Michael dear?

"Yeah, yeah, yeah," Michael sneered at her. Mom punched his shoulder.

"And how was your day?" she asked him.

"Don't ask," Michael said, slamming the car door way too hard.

She turned around to us with raised eyebrows, but

both Free and I chose to look out the window. When we got home, she saw the steps.

"You sweetheart!" she said to Michael, and leaned over and gave him a hug.

"At least that worked out," he said.

Mom looked from Michael to Free and me.

"Why don't you guys go for a nice walk on the beach?"

We didn't argue.

When we came back, they were sitting on the porch, sipping lemonade.

"Time for bed, guys," Mom said. "Brush your teeth. I'll tuck you in later."

From our loft beds I heard them murmuring out there for what seemed like hours, punctuated by chuckles, or one of Michael's laughs. Finally I heard the screen door click open.

"Do you think I scarred them for life?" I heard Michael ask, his voice floating up through the loft window.

"I think you're the one who got scarred," Mom said. Then she giggled.

Chapter 16

The first I heard of Fern was about a week before my birthday. She wasn't even Fern then, just a tropical depression, which sounded to me like some illness you would contract near the equator. In a few days, though, Fern became a storm, and she was heading our way, gathering speed. It had been cloudier than usual, a few cold, drizzly days strung together, but I hadn't thought much about it. We spent little time out on the beach, and it was too yucky to walk to the mainland. I actually felt sorry for the summer people who had picked this week for their big beach vacation. Free and I got cabin fever so bad that Mom gave us money to go play the arcade games. I saw Arthur there for the first time since our trouble at the Beach Bum. He stared at me from across the room and I gave him a little wave, but he just froze up and looked away. He left a few minutes later, and the way he kept his eyes on the ground made me feel sorry for him.

That was when I first heard the word "hurricane" mentioned. The guy we bought tokens from was talking to some sunburned guy with a Massachusetts accent.

"Yup, just got upgraded. She's a real hurricane now. They're calling her Fern. Headed right this way. Could be interesting."

Interesting.

My mother was supremely unworried when I mentioned it to her. "There's always some storm brewing somewhere."

"But what if it hits Fiddle Beach?" I said.

Mom turned the page in her book. It seemed like she had been reading *Gift from the Sea* over again and again. I tried to read it once, but it didn't make much sense to me, so I gave up.

I thought she hadn't heard me, but then she looked up. "Wouldn't be the first time," she said.

I knew that already. I'd seen the pictures at the library taken back in 1954 during Hurricane Carol that showed the waves crashing over the causeway, the little road almost completely under water. I'd seen movies at school of people trying to walk in hurricane winds, and even though they leaned their entire body weight forward, they still had to grab on to things to keep from blowing away. These were adults, full-grown men. Where would Free and I end up?

"But we can't stay here!" I said. It seemed that since her accident, things bothered Mom that shouldn't, and things that should, didn't.

"If landfall is close by, we'll just pack a few things and head inland," she said, still not really paying me any attention.

"But what about all the houses on the beach?"

"Hurricanes are natural, Lise. Houses aren't. You can't fight a hurricane, sweetie."

"But what about my birthday?" My thirteenth birthday was in four days. Just my luck to spend it being blown about.

"It would certainly be a memorable one, wouldn't it?" She was *serious*.

"What about Ben?"

"Ben's house has been there as long as I can remember."

"It looks like toothpicks held together with glue."

She put her book down. Finally.

"You can tell Ben we would be happy take him inland with us if we have to go," she said, after looking at me for a moment.

Fiddle Beach took on a different feel as the wind whipped up. People put wooden shutters over the windows facing the beach, and they covered picture windows with pieces of plywood. All the beach furniture and toys had been collected and stowed away. The coast was empty except for the hard-core beachcombers. No sand games, no near-naked sunbathers. It really looked like the edge of the world. A nuked-out deserted world straight out of some of the science fiction I'd been reading.

Mrs. Lafayette sent her son over to nail plywood over the beachside windows, leaving the lee side windows open so the house wouldn't explode with the change in air pressure. The already gloomy atmosphere inside got darker. The sky was one solid cloud, but there wasn't much rain. Yet. We watched the TV for the weather report, watched the hazy opaque blanket on the weather map creep closer and closer to our coast. Twice, the inactivity got the better of me and I hiked over the breakwater, lonesome for Ben, but he either wasn't home or didn't answer the door.

At first the rain hit us with a shower of tiny pebbles, then like bullets from a machine gun. We sat inside and worked on a puzzle of wild waves crashing on rocks as the ocean crashed outside and the rain crashed on our roof. When we got tired of the puzzle, we each picked up a book, but there was something more comforting about all of us sitting around the kitchen table, close and warm. The first day of rain was okay, novel and new and kind of exciting, but the second day drove me crazy, another day inside, another puzzle, another book. The electricity went out after lunch on the third day, but we had two lanterns, and even though it was early afternoon, we lit them. My mother sat in front of the side window. She stared out at the ocean, which had turned frothy with wind and rain, watching pieces of garbage and sand toys cartwheel by outside, occasionally clunking into our house. Once I looked out and saw someone walking, their yellow slicker inflated with air, billowing out so that they looked like a humongous exotic bird. Babe paced a circle on the floor, and when the wind whined extra loud, he whined with it, high and wavery. Together they sounded like a steel saw working its way through a thick and hard piece of wood. My mother listened to the radio, intermittently at first, and then as the hurricane moved close, she left it on all the time. She was exuberant.

"Isn't this great, guys?" she said. "All this raw fury."

Not, I thought.

Out to sea, the waves built higher, crashing on the beach so hard they felt like tiny earthquakes. Through clear walls of rain the ocean spray looked like smoke, a forest fire at sea during a deluge.

About mid-afternoon I heard a car engine and looked out to see Michael struggling to keep his slicker hood on his head as he made his way toward the house.

"Time to move," he said. My mother looked outside and then back at Michael. I could tell from her expression that she was going to argue, say something stupid about the wild beauty of the storm. So could Michael.

"Annalise, you can do this the easy way or you can do this the hard way. I will tie you up and carry you out if I have to, but you are leaving this house. Now." I was glad one of them had some sense.

Mom opened her mouth.

"It's not negotiable, Annalise," Michael said. Free and I looked at each other.

Mom shut her mouth.

We had already stowed away the glass and

breakables and packed what we needed to take with us, including my birthday presents, so it was a simple matter of collecting Babe's leash and dog food and our library books.

"Save what you can, lose what you must," my mother said with a small smile as she shut the shack door, but I was the only one who heard her. *Good riddance*, I thought. I didn't care if I ever saw that awful place again.

We were practically blown back to Michael's car, where we had trouble opening the doors into the wind. The water was only ten feet from the house when we drove north. There wasn't a house lit on the island or a car in sight on the causeway. We must have been the last ones on Fiddle Beach. If it hadn't been for Michael, I had no doubt we would have toughed out Fern inside that shack, my mother serenely hypnotized by the hum of the wind and the sound of water at her door as we all drowned.

"Is it going to hit us?" I asked.

"Fiddle Beach, probably. Us? No. My house is behind the island, so it's pretty well protected," Michael said. "Landfall should be within a couple of hours, but it might be farther north, which means that the storm surge could hit Fiddle Island at high tide, when the water is already high and close in. That would be messy."

I turned around to throw my backpack over the backseat, and I saw several cardboard boxes under our suitcases. One of the flaps was sticking up, and while most of what I could see was just newspaper-wrapped shapes, a corner of a splint basket protruded from one of the edges.

"What are Ben's things doing in here?" I asked.

"Ben had an appointment at the clinic a few days ago, and he asked if I would take some of his important stuff for safekeeping through the storm. Said they were too heavy for him to carry and asked if I'd stop by and pick them up. So I did."

"When?"

"When what?"

"When did you pick up the boxes?"

"The day he came to the clinic."

"Where is he now?"

Michael shrugged. "I offered to come collect him when the storm got rough, but he said he'd already made other arrangements."

"What kind of arrangements?" I asked.

"They set up evacuation shelters in all the schools. I'm sure he's in one of them."

I was silent. I couldn't see Ben in an evacuation shelter.

"So how is he?" Mom asked. "Healthwise, I mean."

"His eyes are going pretty quickly. I had to tell him he'll be blind within a year. His arthritis bothers him. His attitude, however, is always good. I wish some of my other patients were as positive. That man can find the bright side of anything."

"So what's the bright side of blindness?" I asked, thinking of the close watch he kept on his world.

"Not having to see the garbage on the beach, he said." Michael laughed, but a shiver went through me.

"He's no fool, Lise," Mom said. "He can smell a bad storm before anyone."

"He said he wouldn't be surprised if this is the one that finally takes the bird house," Michael agreed. "That's why I've got his stuff."

"And then where will he go?" I asked.

"I told him I could get him into an assisted living facility," Michael said. "He's been on his own out there way too long, anyway. It will be a blessing for him, really, after he adjusts."

"And he agreed to that?" I asked.

"Of course. He knows the score," Michael said.

Yes, Ben knew the score.

"He gave me something for you," Michael said. "It's for your birthday, but I guess this is close enough." He leaned over to the glove compartment and opened it. He withdrew a small box and handed it to me. Inside, on a pad of deer hide, was Ben's shark tooth necklace.

Everyone oohed and aahed. I sat in silence, feeling very cold. I could see the shark tooth against Ben's neck, could see him reach up as he talked, touching it, feeling its smoothness.

Ben hadn't gone to a shelter.

We drove into Michael's garage, and they began unloading the car. Michael's neighborhood still had electricity, and the house didn't seem nearly as gray and bleak as ours. I looked through the window of the door that led to the side yard, and could just make out the breakwater in the distance. I watched Mom, Michael, and Free go into the house, and then took my chance, quietly opening the door that led outside. But not quietly enough. Free stopped on the stairs that led into the house and turned to look at me, his brow furrowed.

"It's okay," I said, slipping the shark tooth necklace on. "I'll be back real quick." Free's eyes widened, and I realized my voice was a little shaky. I saw a coil of rope resting in the corner by Michael's boat and picked it up, slinging it over my shoulder. You never know.

I slipped out the door. I put my head down into the wind and started to run.

Chapter 17

And then the rain really let loose. Buckets of rain. I'd heard the phrase before but never understood it until now. You might as well have thrown a bucket of water at me, or tossed me into a swimming pool. My hair separated into nasty dripping snakes, and I was wet to my underwear in a second, in spite of my slicker. The wind blew the rain every which way and it didn't matter if I ran facing backward or forward, the water pelted me like popping popcorn. Although inland, Michael's house was almost directly in line with the breakwater, and it would take me less time to get to the breakwater on foot than it had taken us to drive from our house to Michael's. I ran through the weird yellow light toward the shore, stopping only when I absolutely couldn't breathe anymore. There was nobody on the street as I ran.

I knew Ben was all alone on the island now that we had left. Or maybe I was completely wrong and Ben was sitting in a shelter, sipping hot tea and telling fortunes, the gap in his teeth revealed by his smile. Ben was safe and warm and dry and I was miserable, and when I made my way back to my family, Free would stare at me with accusing, silent eyes. And then my mom would kill me for worrying her. And Michael would probably help her.

It wasn't late, but it was quite dark now and the wind howled. I'd read in books that wind howled, and I always wondered how air could actually do that. Well, this wind did, high and sad and unforgiving. I wound the rope around my waist so I could use my hands and crouch low to climb onto the top of the breakwater. The wind was so strong that I dropped quickly down the north side to gain shelter. Since the hurricane was moving in from the south, the breakwater would give me some protection until I got to the fiddle neck. Then I could cross over the breakwater and hop down the south side to get to Ben's.

The only problem was, there was no fiddle neck. The entire sandbar south of the breakwater was underwater. I braced myself and went over the top of the breakwater on my belly, using hands and feet to advance against the gale, and down the other side, where the wind was tremendous. I looked around until I found a thick stick that had washed up on the rocks. Scooting down low close to the waterline, I stuck it in every few feet to test the depth of the water. Finally my stick touched relatively solid sand and, ankle-deep in the sea, I moved slowly away from the breakwater toward where I thought Ben's house should be. I couldn't see his blue bird house, but I saw a little glimmer, like a weak lantern in a small window. Ben would never leave a lit lantern in an empty house.

I began to run but tripped and did a belly flop in the ever-deepening water, soaked through with both rain and salt water now. I picked myself up and felt the pull of a strong, strange current. Perhaps these waves could carry me to Ben's even faster than I could run, and in a few minutes I would take Ben's hand and tell him that it wasn't his time to die. I would tell him that I didn't care about the bone harpoons or baskets, but I cared about him. And if his house got destroyed, I was sure my mom would let him live with us, because that's the kind of person my mom is.

I would tell him all of this and if that didn't work, then I would tell him what I had never told anyone else. That I was afraid my father had left because of me, that because of me, my mother had had to choose between having Free and having my dad. Other dads had the time and money and energy for more than one kid, so what was different about him? This: He had me. Me. It was my fault. I would tell Ben that after my dad left, I was terrified that Mom might decide that she didn't have the time, the money, or the energy either and leave me too. That since she'd had the accident, it felt a little like she had left. And then I would tell Ben he couldn't leave me too, he just couldn't.

Except the waves were pushing me away from Ben.

I stood up again, in hip-deep water now, but my feet were pulled from beneath me, as if someone were playing a joke. With the next wave I had to struggle to keep my head above water, and the water was cold, colder than I had ever felt. I should have been wearing my wet suit. For once in my life I voluntarily let my feet lose their grip on what Michael called my terra firma. I would float, I would swim, I would brave what lay beneath, whatever it took to get to Ben. I fixed my eyes on the lantern's small light, that one dry warm spot in my world, and I kicked. I reached and pulled and kicked for all I was worth.

And I almost made it. From thirty feet or so, I could see that the water was more than halfway up the bird house stilts, and through the window where the light was shining, I saw Ben sitting in his chair. He sat very still, fingers laced, his black hair loose and long. He was staring not at me but out his window to the sea, his lips moving slightly. He wore his great beaded robe, and probably his leggings and moccasins as well. But for his lips moving, he could have been sleeping. At that moment the wind seemed to die down just so I could yell for him.

"Ben!" I shrieked, but water filled my mouth.

"Ben!" I tried again, knowing that if he saw me he would be forced to come back with me, to stay in this life a little longer. I knew he wouldn't let me die. Soon I would be close enough for him to hear me and, roped together, we would paddle to safety, cold to the bone but safe, back to my family.

But the next wave dunked me, and when I came up I heard a horrible sound. Part animal, part magic, the sound of wood wrenching and tearing and splitting, and I saw the little flicker of the lantern nailed to Ben's table wobble. It wobbled, then held steady, but lower, and I realized that Ben's stilt house was leaning toward the sea. At least one of its front stilts had splintered and buckled, and the others were groaning under the uneven weight.

"Ben!" I yelled as loudly as I could, so loudly that my voice shook in my chest and my throat felt cut. But Ben stared straight ahead, his lips still moving.

Another wave hit me, and the last thing I saw was Ben's chair on the move, sliding and slipping across the floor of that tiny cabin toward the sea, with Ben in it. I went under and felt myself tossed, twisted, and thrown beneath a blanket of water. Even though I kept my eyes open, I could see nothing but black, could feel nothing but cold, fluid death as it pressed on me and made me dance. I burst to the top, gasping and mad, but was brought up short by a vision of pure nothing. No Ben, no lantern, no cabin. Thinking maybe I had been swept so far out to sea that Ben's house was behind me, I turned to look the other way.

Nothing.

I looked to each side. Still nothing. And then I spotted it. A small peaked roof, drifting low, moving toward the open sea end of the breakwater. Ben's blue roof. I struck a course to it, but the next wave hit me hard, and when I came up, the roofline was gone, simply gone. Surely Ben had escaped and was treading water with me, or floating if he couldn't tread water. I looked all around and thought I saw Ben coming slowly, steadily toward me, but when that dark image came into focus, it was just a piece of timber. Blue painted timber.

Another huge wave crashed over me. I tasted blood, then seawater, and felt the tang of salt in an open wound and knew my lip was split. As the wave receded, I felt myself pulled off the bar out toward the angry sea, and I swam hard against it to get back to semisolid ground. With relief I felt one of the submerged boulders of the sandbar in front of me; but when I stood up, the water was up to my armpits. I needed to rest, so I crawled up on the rock and pulled my legs to my chest for warmth. It was then that I realized that the real pull of the water wasn't out to sea but toward the tall and cruel rocky wall of the breakwater.

The next wave was so enormous that I was too stunned to dive under it, and it hit me hard, knocking me off and slamming me against the rock as I twisted in the water. The knifelike barnacles tore my bare hands as I tried to hold on to the rock. My teeth felt jagged against my tongue, and I spit out broken pieces of tooth. Arms of water grabbed me and I felt my feet lose contact with solid beach as I was pulled away from my rock, but this time, pulled under as well. I heard screaming and knew it was my own voice, but I could not stop. I screamed and screamed because as long as I was screaming I knew I was alive.

The cold was even worse than the bone-crushing power of the waves. I remembered Michael telling me that the only thing you had to worry about in the water here was the cold. My head hit a rock with the next wave, cutting off my scream. Lights exploded in my head. I was going to die with my own screaming in my ears and queer lights in my eyes. But not yet.

I foundered for purchase on the rocks, but my tennis shoes slipped against the wet algae. I tied the rope as best I could around my waist, and I tried to loop the rope around my rock to keep myself from being dragged, but my hands were too cold and shredded to make the rope behave. I noted with an odd detachment that my rain jacket had been sliced by the barnacles and was smeared with blood. I couldn't believe I was still wearing it—the pockets and the arms were filled with water, weighing me down. I stripped it off as quickly as I could, given that my arms and fingers weren't working very well. Choking on seaweed and seawater and whatever else was roiling around in that awful stew, I raked my hands over the slimy rock and felt the pain of cut flesh and knew I could not hold on through the next wave. I breathed silently, no air left to scream.

I shook my head to clear it, but the lights remained. They bobbled up and down, two of them, no, three. They came not from my head this time but from where the shore met the breakwater. I heard shouts in the lull before the next wave broke over my head. Just before the water filled my ears, I heard a small clear voice I had never heard before. It was calling my name.

When I tried to breathe again, water filled my nose instead of air. The ragged waves pulled me off the sandbar again, away from the rock this time. I gagged and inhaled sharply, but felt only water in my nose. I could not even scream now, and my flailing arms and legs found nothing to save me.

I felt a sharp pressure at my side, then painful pinching at my arm. My head rose above the water and my lungs sucked wildly at the sudden air. I felt rather than saw a body near me, and when I reached out I felt wet, thick fur, and I felt sorry for all the poor harbor seals caught in this storm that were being battered about just like me. Then I heard a familiar whining in my ear, and my loose hand brushed flippers much longer than a harbor seal's. Babe! He had me by the arm and was struggling to push me up through the surf. I grabbed his back, pulling him under, and heard him gargle as he, too, inhaled salt water. I let go and felt myself sink again, but the rope around my waist floated up and grazed my cheek. The rope! Babe found my forearm beneath the sea somehow and pulled me up once more. This time, rather than grabbing his back, I put the rope in his mouth. He clamped down on it.

"Go on, Babe! Pull! Harder!" I yelled. The big dog whined and struggled, and I felt the rope pull taut. I could barely use my arms and legs to keep my head above water, and Babe didn't seem to be making much progress. I had come for Ben and failed; now Babe had come for me, and he, too, would come to rest at the bottom of the deep sea. It seemed so unfair for three of us to die so cold and alone. I heard Ben's words:

"We're all part of the plan."

"What if I don't like the plan?" I'd replied.

"Sometimes you can bend it a little, but you have to know when to fight for what is important to you, and when to accept the plan."

It dawned on me through my numbness that if Babe was here, my mother and Michael and Free must have come as well. The people at the edge of the sea were important to me, and they were at the edge of the sea because I was important to them and they were willing to fight for me. The lights had been theirs, the voice my brother's. Free talking! Calling my name! I forced my cold and deadweight limbs to beat back the swirling sea; I tried to move forward to help Babe help me. I strained hard to see the lights again, and yes, they were still there. They had not given up, and neither would I. Babe whined beside me, and I yelled toward the dim but steady light. I kicked and flailed against the harsh water, I spit back the sea. I focused solely on the lights, and as one connected unit Babe and I struggled toward them. At times it seemed as if we stayed still and made no progress at all against the suck of a retreating wave; other times we caught the top of a wave and rode it closer to shore, although we were carried closer and closer to the breakwater as well. The water and wind stung my face, but as I squinted into the dark, I could still see three lights. Then another huge wave crashed over us, and when I surfaced I saw only two lights clustered together. Babe and I were dangerously close to the wall of rocks now, but my strength was almost gone and it seemed more important to get to something solid, anything, than to avoid the rocks. I saw the third light rise from the sea in front of me, closer now. I heard a voice call my name, but when I tried to answer back, nothing came from my frozen, exhausted lungs. Babe barked once, twice. The rope slipped from his mouth when he barked, and I felt the sea pull me back. I was shivering hard now, and I felt the shooting pains in my arms and legs that my mother had warned me about.

"No!" I screamed angrily. My head slipped beneath the surface of the sea, and I gathered the last of my strength to push toward the surface.

"Don't leave me!" I shrieked to Babe.

"I'm not going to leave you," the light yelled back, about ten feet from me. "I've got you."

But the light didn't have me at all. A wave came

and I felt myself slammed into another submerged rock, knocking the wind out of me. I heard a thud and a yell beside me, and then a strong hand closed on my arm just as the receding wave tried to pull me back. I looked up into Michael's face illuminated by his headlamp, his cheek cut by the barnacles, his knuckles ripped and bleeding, his face drawn in pain, his other arm holding his side.

"Where's Babe?" I asked.

"I don't know. I found you because he barked, but I haven't seen him."

"Babe," I yelled. "Babe!"

"We have to leave him, Lise."

I would have argued more, but I could see that Michael was hurt. He reached for the rope still around my waist.

"We need to ride the waves in as close to the breakwater as we dare. Swim only against the back pull of the waves, to save your strength. Once we get to the breakwater, the rocks will keep us from getting pulled out, and we can crawl along the breakwater to shore." He pointed toward an oncoming wave and looped my rope around his wrist. "Go for it!"

It took five waves to get us close enough to use the

breakwater as protection. Funny how something you thought might kill you could save you after all. After the fifth wave Michael was on solid ground, although the water was still up to his thighs. He scrambled toward shore, and the rope that connected us took me with him. I watched Michael disappear around a large rock, and he pulled me in after him just as the next wave crashed over us. Water poured down on us from above, and even with Michael crouching over me I thought I was going to die from the pressure and the cold. The second the wave relented, Michael was up and moving toward the next haven. I could hear him grunt with exertion, but the tension on the rope never let up. A red flashing light joined the other two lights, and I heard the eerie wail of a siren. I heard voices calling for us, but neither Michael nor I had enough wind to answer. Eleven more times we sneaked up the breakwater in between the battering waves, and still the lights seemed far away.

"It's not so deep now. We must be on the shore. This is it! Even if a wave hits, try and stay on your feet." Michael was breathing oddly and the blood on his face scared me, but I nodded. I didn't have the strength to speak.

The wave crested and Michael headed out away from the rocks, and soon I was up to mid-thigh in the icy sea. My legs felt like solid concrete, and but for the rope around my waist I would have sunk to my knees. I concentrated on dragging one frozen foot in front of the other, on not letting the current pull my legs from beneath me. The lights came closer in agonizingly slow motion, and then I saw before me, some ways away yet, an oddly lit patch of sand. Clear and rockless sand. It looked almost sunny, and soft, very soft. There was no wind anymore, no rain, no waves, no pain, there was nothing at all for me except that patch of beach. That patch of beach was warm and dry and safe, and I was going to make it there. I knew very clearly and with great certainty that I was not going to die in the sea, that as long as I wore my shark tooth, the ocean could do me no harm.

I saw Michael stumble in the water in front of me and fall face-first. Then I felt myself being gently carried past him, like a delicate and fragile sand dollar. The last thing I heard was barking.

Chapter 18

My face felt as if it had been inflated almost to bursting, a big skin balloon. There was a solid core of pain surrounded by stinging, tingling smaller pains. I gingerly brought my hand up to my mouth and felt enormous lips, lips the size of hot dogs.

"Oh!" I said, or tried to, but it came out more like "Unh." Free's face appeared over me, smiling.

"She's awake!" he crowed. It was a sweet voice, a clear voice, with crisp and clear words. *Burnt toast,* I thought out of nowhere. I started to giggle, then stopped. It hurt.

My mother's face loomed above me, but I couldn't read the expression very well. Joy and love, as always, but something else I had never seen—fear, perhaps? My mother wasn't afraid of anything, was she?

"Where's Michael?" I tried to sit but my muscles didn't want to work. Sharp twinges of pain exploded everywhere. "Where's Babe?"

"Imagine that—I rate above the dog," Michael said. His head slowly came into focus over me, and he moved stiffly as if he, too, hurt. His face was no longer smeared with blood, but long, ugly cuts lined his forehead and cheeks. I turned my head toward him and I could see his arm was in a sling. Some kind of tape or bandage was visible through the open neck of his shirt.

"Are you okay?" I asked.

"I'm the doctor. That's my line."

"He broke two ribs," Mom said. "And bruised his shoulder pretty badly."

I turned my head carefully. I was in a hospital room, wrapped in blankets.

"What's the matter with me?"

"Aside from a probable concussion and being shredded by barnacles and submerged in a frigid sea for a while, not much," Michael said.

"Boy, are you ugly," Free said. I realized that some things would be different now that my brother was talking. I wasn't really surprised: Mom always said he would speak when he was ready.

"Do you know your teeth are broken?" Free asked.

My hand flew to my mouth and I remembered the sharp pain, the rough craggy edges. My beautiful teeth. I wondered if someone might find them washed up on the beach like tiny pearly shells.

"It's okay," Mom said, "it will make you more interesting. Interesting is always better than perfect."

"And Babe?" Although I wasn't sure I wanted to know.

"Babe's asleep. Has been for over twelve hours. We can't budge him from the car."

"What happened?"

"You tell us. We were moving things into the house, when we discovered you were gone. Free guessed where you'd gone. I couldn't believe it, but he was quite adamant. And he was right. You know the rest."

"Did Ben die?"

My mom didn't respond immediately, but she looked at me steadily.

"Yes, I believe he did, Lise. He hasn't shown up at any of the shelters."

"Why did he do that?"

"It made sense to him, Lise. Even though we'd all rather have him here with us, we have to respect his choice."

I knew she was right. I'd known it from the

beginning. I'd been thinking only of what I wanted when I went back to Ben's, not what Ben wanted. *It's easy to convince yourself that you're right, when really you're just being selfish.* I'd nearly killed Michael. And Babe.

I looked at Michael. What a mess his face was. He had left the safe shore to come after someone he hadn't even known two months earlier. Without Babe and without Michael, I would not be hurting right now. I would be in no pain, absolutely no pain at all. "I'm not going to leave you," he'd said. And he hadn't.

"Why did you come after me?" I asked Michael.

He looked at me like I'd asked something really stupid.

"Why?" Then he looked at my mother and shook his head.

I knew that if he hadn't been there, it would have been my mother coming after me. And then Free would have been left alone in a world that didn't understand him. I knew this was true. Free knew it too. He crawled gently into Michael's lap, careful not to bump his sling.

"Happy birthday, Lise," Free said.

The sea takes away, but the sea gives. It took away Ben that night, but it gave me back, burped me up like a rejected piece of garbage to be incorporated into one of our beach sculptures. I was spared not because Babe was strong or Michael's timing was perfect, but because the sea relented at the last minute and simply let me go. I wonder, though, if the love that brought my family to the edge was so powerful that it shook me loose from the grip of the cold roll and pull of the waves, that the ocean knew when it was beat. *I'm not going to leave you.* When I told my mother about that crystalline calm moment when I saw the illuminated beach and knew for certain that I was going to live, she was quiet for a moment. She stroked the hair away from my eyes, and then she nodded, smiling.

"Moments of grace are very special," she said.

Fern wasn't a huge hurricane, as hurricanes go: a Category One with wind speeds of up to eighty-five miles an hour, five inches of rain. "Poorly organized" was the term I heard used, which reminded me of a messy desk. Fern had weakened as she neared the coast, pulling cool dry air from a front coming down from the north. She never did make landfall. Instead, she changed her mind, veered back out to sea, and just fizzled out. She was bad enough, however, and I wonder where Fiddle Beach would be if Fern had gotten herself "organized." Where I'd be. Our ratty little shack was not only still standing after all that, it looked pretty much the same. It had flooded, of course, but nothing seemed the worse for wear. It actually smelled better than it had before.

The breakwater took the brunt of Fern's force, just like it was supposed to. Our little house was well protected by it, but a lot of the fancy summer houses needed some major repairs. I wondered about the person who'd built our shack. Now, there was someone who knew how to build a sand castle, I bet.

There were a lot of neat things that Fern spewed up on the beach, and we had awesome garbage sculptures for the next few days. But the most amazing things were the hundreds of tiny sand dollars, none bigger than a nickel, that washed up on the shore. Most of them appeared on the south side of the breakwater, near where Ben's house used to be, floating like trusting little boats on top of the water, then gently letting themselves rest on the sand when the tide went out. Free and I collected them by the handful, and my mother layered them gently in a clear glass bowl. Ben would have loved to see those delicate tiny survivors.

Fern had eaten the sand dunes like they were cotton candy. New inlets had been carved, old ones filled in. Wind-driven sand and sea salt had etched house paint, car paint, tree bark. Ben's house was gone, of course, and the hurricane had dumped so much new sand on the beach south of the breakwater that you couldn't even see the broken stilts. It bothered me that something so real and familiar could disappear so completely, so I carried a shovel over the breakwater one morning and began to dig. While I was digging, silhouettes appeared on top of the breakwater, and soon Arthur and Beth and Free were beside me, silently rooting in the sand. It took us a couple of tries to find the right area, but we finally hit shredded wood. After the first post, it was easy to find the rest. I watched as the tide filled in our hard work with sand, sand, and more sand, and I felt quieter and less sad than I had since Ben left. That's how I think of it. He left. At first I thought that I'd lost him, but then I realized that after you find someone, really find them, you never lose them. He was right; part of him will always belong to this world. And part of him will always belong to me.

I no longer believe the sea means to hurt me. I know this the way we know the most important things: I just know. The ocean is what it is. Like life, like luck, it can be cruel, it can be merciful. And I know that while the murmur of the ocean waves is the voice of our deepest fears, its whispers also speak of who we are and who we wish to be. I am still learning who I am, but I no longer wish to be someone limited by my fears. I have taken up windsurfing, although Michael says I can still call myself an edge person if I want to. And I wear Ben's shark tooth necklace all the time.

There are often two silhouettes down at the waterline in the evening now, low voices that rise and fall with the magic chant of the waves. My mother still patrols the beach, not even using a crutch anymore, a garbage bag slung over her shoulder. She still limps a little and probably always will. The sun has streaked her hair so light that I can no longer see the gray. People turn to watch her still, not because she limps, but because she is so beautiful and strong. They see her lips moving when she is all alone and they may think that she is muttering crazy, witchy thoughts, but I know that she is singing.

1-4169-3598-3 (paperback)

0-689-83957-X (hardcover)
0-689-83958-8 (paperback)

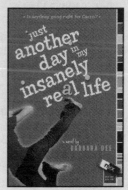

1-4169-0861-7 (hardcover)
1-4169-4739-6 (paperback)

1-4169-3519-3 (paperback)

1-4169-4893-7 (paperback)

1-4169-0930-3 (hardcover)
1-4169-0931-1 (paperback)

From 2-time Newbery Medalist
E. L. KONIGSBURG

*The Outcasts of
19 Schuyler Place*
0-689-86637-2

*From the Mixed-Up Files of
Mrs. Basil E. Frankweiler*
NEWBERY MEDAL WINNER
0-689-71181-6

The View from Saturday
NEWBERY MEDAL WINNER
0-689-81721-5

*Jennifer, Hecate, Macbeth,
William McKinley, and Me, Elizabeth*
NEWBERY HONOR BOOK
1-4169-4829-5

Altogether, One at a Time
1-4169-5501-1

*A Proud Taste for Scarlet
and Miniver*
0-689-84624-X

(george)
1-4169-4957-7

The Second Mrs. Gioconda
0-689-82121-2

My Father's Daughter
1-4169-5500-3

Throwing Shadows
1-4169-4959-3

Journey to an 800 Number
1-4169-5875-4

Silent to the Bone
0-689-83602-3

Aladdin Paperbacks • Simon & Schuster Children's Publishing
www.SimonSaysKids.com